The Alternate History

© 2001 by The Kent State University Press, Kent, Ohio 44242
All rights reserved
Library of Congress Catalog Card Number 00-062024
ISBN 0-87338-683-3
Manufactured in the United States of America

06 05 04 03 02 01   5 4 3 2 1

Library of Congress Cataloging-in-Publication Data
Hellekson, Karen, 1966–
   The alternate history:refiguring historical time / Karen Hellekson.
      p.   cm.
   Includes bibliographical references (p.) and index.
   ISBN 0-87338-683-3 (alk. paper) ∞
      1. Historical fiction, American—History and criticism. 2. Literature and history—
   United States—History—20th century. 3. American fiction—20th century—History
   and criticism. 4. Science fiction, American—History and criticism. 5. Aldiss, Brian
   Wilson, 1925– Malacia tapestry. 6. Moore, Ward, 1903– Bring the jubilee. 7. Dick,
   Philip K. Man in the high castle. 8. History—Errors, inventions, etc. 9. Time travel
   in literature. 10. History in literature. 11. Time in literature. I. Title.

   PS374.H5 H44   2001
   813'.0876209358—dc21   00-062024

Part of the introduction was published as "Toward a Taxonomy of the Alternate History
Genre," *Extrapolation* 41 (2000): 248–56. A much different version of part of chapter 2 was
presented as *"Bring the Jubilee* as First Contact," Frontiers in the American Imagination,
Augustana College, Rock Island, Illinois, March 1995. A portion of chapter 3 was presented
as "H. Beam Piper's *Lord Kalvan of Otherwhen:* Parallel Worlds and Agency," Great Plains
Popular Culture Association/American Culture Association annual meeting, with the Center
for Great Plains Studies' 22d Annual Interdisciplinary Symposium, Lincoln, Nebraska, April
1998. Part of chapter 4 was presented as *"The Man in the High Castle* and Temporality,"
Science Fiction Research Association annual meeting, Eau Claire, Wisconsin, June 1996. A
portion of chapter 6 was presented as "Brian Aldiss's *The Malacia Tapestry:* Science Fiction
and Change," Midwest Modern Language Association convention, Minneapolis, Minnesota,
November 1996. And much of chapter 7 was published as "Poul Anderson's Time Patrol as
Anti–Alternate History," *Extrapolation* 37 (1996): 234–44, and is reprinted with permission of
The Kent State University Press.

British Library Cataloging-in-Publication data are available.

The Alternate History

Refiguring Historical Time

Karen Hellekson

THE KENT STATE
UNIVERSITY PRESS
Kent, Ohio, & London

Contents

Acknowledgments

Thanks to James Gunn, Cheryl Lester, Joe Harrington, Philip Baringer, Edgar V. McKnight Jr., Robert Schmunk, Mike K. Johnson, Rachel Hile Bassett, and the staff at the Kenneth Spencer Research Library at the University of Kansas, Lawrence.

Introduction

In his introduction to *Three Trips in Time and Space* (1973), Robert Silverberg writes, "If all things are possible, if all gates stand open, what sort of world will we have?" (6). As a genre, the alternate history—the branch of literature that concerns itself with history's turning out differently than what we know to be true—attempts to answer this question. *Refiguring Historical Time: The Alternate History* is the result of my long-standing interest in both science fiction and history. Using primarily novel-length alternate histories by science fiction genre writers, I perform close readings of exemplar texts that explore the alternate history in terms of historiography and analyses of narrative for two reasons: to show how the classification system I have devised for organizing alternate histories works, and to show that the the best kind of alternate history is the one concerned most intimately with plausible causal relationships.

When I began reading the work of scholars concerned with time, I found that notions of narrative were intimately bound with expressions of time. I could not separate the two. Paul Ricoeur and Hayden White in particular allow me to discuss time and narrative meaningfully. Ricoeur argues that narrative is not reality but rather the way we organize our temporal experience. Ricoeur also puts together time as experienced by people with time as measured by devices such as calendars and clocks, arguing that narrated time links these two ways of structuring time. In *Metahistory*, White argues that historians write history not as disinterested outsiders but as interested parties who structure their narratives, perhaps

1

unconsciously, tropologically in order to make a particular point. Using categorizations of emplotment modes (via Northrop Frye), ideological positions (via Karl Mannheim), and paradigms of form (via Stephen C. Pepper), White makes the historian a creator who fits together, consciously or unconsciously, various modes that will allow the historian to construct a true story. Like Ricoeur, White blurs the boundaries between fiction and history, between creative writer and historian. This theory—that fiction and history are both constructed from language and do not differ except in the truth-claim of the text—is known as "narrativism" (Zagorin, 14). Chapter 1 discusses history and narrative in more detail.

To unify the discussion, I place it within the larger framework of four models of history: the eschatological, genetic, entropic, and teleological models. This is the first study to analyze the alternate history using historical and narrative terms. The four models of history play with beginning and end, design and disorder. These models are useful in contextualizing my discussion and are not necessarily used overtly in historical discourse. The eschatological model of history is concerned with final events or an ultimate destiny, be it the ultimate destiny of humankind or of history. Its opposite is genetic history, or history concerned with origin, development, or cause. The entropic model of history assumes that the process of history is one of disorder or randomness. Its opposite is teleological or future-oriented history, history that seems to have a design or purpose. Though the alternate history may focus on any of these four models, as a genre, the alternate history fundamentally concerns itself with the genesis of history; this is one reason why three of my text-based chapters focus on this model. The genetic model lies at the heart of every alternate history because the alternate history relies on cause and effect. It assumes that an event in the past caused our present. However, some alternate histories have pervasive themes that rely on eschatological, entropic, or teleological models of history. In many ways, this break from the expected focus on the genetic model results in a refreshing change of concerns. I have one chapter each on these three models of history. However, I argue that the genetic model is the best one for articulating the concerns that the alternate history, as a genre, deals with.

Alternate histories revolve around the basic premise that some event in the past did not occur as we know it did, and thus the present has changed. Philip K. Dick's *The Man in the High Castle* (1962), perhaps the best known of all alternate histories, creates a world in which the Axis powers won World War II. Dick explores what the West Coast would be like if occupied by the Japanese, from changing speech patterns to pedicabs to slavery. Sometimes alternate histories rely on time travel, as do Poul Anderson's Time Patrol stories. Anderson has invented policemen who can make sure history happens as it ought to: they have the ability to travel back and forth in time, righting wrongs and battling evildoers who want to change the future by altering the past. The parallel worlds story is also a kind of alternate history, but one in which a number of alternate histories exist simultaneously. Characters, by means of sophisticated machines or bizarre accident, can move from one alternate history to another. The best-known texts of this kind are H. Beam Piper's Paratime short stories and his Paratime novel *Lord Kalvan of Otherwhen* (1965), itself made up of several previously published novelettes and novellas.

Alternate histories are also known as alternative histories, alternate universes, allohistories, or uchronias. One scholar, Joerg Helbig, prefers the term *parahistory*. Historians use the term *counterfactual*. Although the term *alternative history* seems to be preferred among scholars (and it has the benefit of grammatical correctness), writers and editors like the term *alternate history*, as evidenced by book titles such as Mike Resnick's and Mike Resnick and Martin H. Greenberg's string of Alternate anthologies, including *Alternate Outlaws* (1994), *Alternate Presidents* (1992), *Alternate Warriors* (1993), and *Alternate Tyrants* (1997). Some anthologists do use the term *alternative*, of course, notably Robert Adams's anthology *Alternatives*. Although I prefer the term *alternative* in solidarity with these writers, I do so because the term *alternative history* has another meaning among historians: histories that approach their subject from a nonstandard position. Historians or literary critics who analyze the Italian Renaissance from a woman's point of view are practicing a kind of alternative history. I use other terms for the sake of variety; by so doing, I am not implying any subtle differentiations among kinds of alternate histories.

Science fiction asks, "What if the world were somehow different?" This question is at the center of both science fiction and the alternate history. Answering this question in fictive texts creates science fiction or other fantastic texts, including fantasy and magic realism. One important point I wish to stress is that the alternate history is a subgenre of the genre of science fiction, which is itself a subgenre of fantastic (that is, not realistic) literature. Science fiction writer and alternate historian Harry Harrison remarks that the alternate history story, or the "speculative-development-thought-story," "is the very essence of what science fiction is all about" (Harrison, "Worlds," 114). The alternate history is persuasively science fictional: it uses history as the moment of what Darko Suvin calls "estrangement" that is common to all science fiction. Suvin notes, "We can divide prose literature into naturalistic and estranged genres, according to whether they endeavour to faithfully reproduce textures, surfaces and relationships vouched for by human senses and common sense, or turn their attention to empirically unknown locations for the new relationships shown in the narration" (*Positions*, 34); Suvin argues that science fiction does the latter. I do not want to get bogged down in a long description of science fiction as a literary genre, and better people than I have attempted definitions of science fiction and failed miserably. For a short overview of the definition of science fiction, I direct the reader to the entry entitled "Definitions of sf" in *The Encyclopedia of Science Fiction*, edited by John Clute and Peter Nicholls.

The alternate history relies on the same articulations of change evident in history. Science fiction, though a literature of the fantastic, is rule bound. It sets up rules it wants to follow and then follows them, using some rules of the universe (black holes, gravity) but breaking others for the sake of plot convenience (faster-than-light travel, alien life). Science fiction plays within boundaries of physical law, even if the writer sometimes makes up the laws. One such boundary that science fiction does not tend to subvert is that of history and change: the movement from past to present, in terms of historical development or of evolution, is taken as a given. Even fiction that deals with time travel, wormholes in time and space, or other singular events that rupture the fabric of time acknowledges the movement from past to present to future and the role of cause and effect in that movement, even if one can move outside the present.

Science fiction critics are quick to point out that science fiction is a genre intimately concerned with history. Darko Suvin notes that "the understanding of SF—constituted by history and evaluated in history—is doubly impossible without a sense of history and its possibilities, a sense that this genre is a system which changes in the process of social history" (*Positions*, 45). Robert H. Canary notes that "science fiction's implicit claim to operate by the same rules as historical reality means that it is inevitably speculating about the nature of those rules" (166). Here, I argue that a historical sensibility can be usefully brought to bear on a particular branch of science fiction.

The alternate history's use of changed historical points to bring about different realities is, I think, a case parallel to science fiction's use of extrapolations of current events to bring about fictive futures. Dominick LaCapra, speaking of fantasy, notes, "These forms of 'otherness' or alterity may prove to have unexpected transformative implications" (5). In fact, the alternate history rewrites history and reality, thus transforming the world and our understanding of reality. These texts change the present by transforming the past.

The alternate history as a genre speculates about such topics as the nature of time and linearity, the past's link to the present, the present's link to the future, and the role of individuals in the history-making process. Alternate histories question the nature of history and of causality;

they question accepted notions of time and space; they rupture linear movement; and they make readers rethink their world and how it has become what it is. They are a critique of the metaphors we use to discuss history. And they foreground the "constructedness" of history and the role narrative plays in this construction.

I have divided the alternate history into several different classifications that I refer to in the rest of this text. These groupings link different kinds of alternate histories according to the nature of the historical inquiry, not according to the nature of the story told. I do not link together all alternate histories that focus on World War II, for example, simply because they share a common event.

William Joseph Collins describes what he calls a "taxonomy" of alternate history. He divides the alternate history into four major divisions, as follows: (1) the "pure uchronia," which implies an alternate history alone without allowing for any other reality; (2) the "plural uchronia," which places the alternative reality next to that of the reader; (3) "infinite presents," or parallel worlds stories; and (4) "time-travel alteration," which has travelers moving from their present to the past to alter events (85–86). Collins therefore divides his alternate histories into categories based on the subject's position.

My own divisions, which point to the moment of the break rather than the subject's position, are as follows: (1) the nexus story, which includes time-travel–time-policing stories and battle stories; (2) the true alternate history, which may include alternate histories that posit different physical laws; and (3) the parallel worlds story. Nexus stories occur at the moment of the break. The true alternate history occurs after the break, sometimes a long time after. And the parallel worlds story implies that there was no break—that all events that could have occurred did occur. I divide the alternate history into these categories because I see the alternate history as querying historical concerns about time, including the notion of sequence that is so integral to the concept of time. There are so many different kinds of alternate histories that I had to limit myself to ones I felt really queried historicity.

The nexus story is an alternate history that focuses on a crucial point in history, such as a battle or assassination, in which something different happens that changes the outcome. I call this crucial point or happening a "nexus event." The changed event need not be something historically significant or big; in fact, sometimes the most interesting alternate histories are those that explore worlds radically other that resulted from an extremely minor or forgotten event that snowballed. Philosophers and historians call the "if–then" question, when the "then" part of the question is false, a "counterfactual conditional" (Bulhof, 146). Johannes Bulhof argues that "counterfactual conditionals are an essential ingredient in the ascription of causality" (155). All alternate histories, of course, play with cause and effect by presenting a counterfactual conditional. In nexus stories, the "then" of the "if–then" question is in play. I borrow the term *nexus* from Poul Anderson, many of whose stories deal with meddlings around nexus events. As a condition of the fictional world they are creating, science fiction authors usually make it difficult for changes in nexus events to occur, thus limiting the scope of causality (and making for a more manageable text). Poul Anderson, for instance, in his Time Patrol works, notes: "The continuum does tend to maintain its structure. A radical change is only possible at certain critical points in history. Elsewhen, compensations occur" (*Shield of Time*, 168). Anderson thus limits changes in history to these nexus points. These "critical points," often battles, are the focus of the nexus story. Though William Joseph Collins and other critics use the term *Jonbar hinge* (Collins, 175–76) for what I call a "nexus event," I find their term confusing and unwieldy; it certainly is not immediately understood by those who don't get the in-joke. These critics borrow the term from a utopian civilization in Jack Williamson's *The Legion of Time* (1938), a text that creates a utopia warring with a dystopia, only one of which will come to be if the protagonist makes a particular choice as a child. The protagonist frustrates both groups by making a third, totally unexpected, choice.

There are two subsets of the nexus story: the time-travel–time-policing story and the battle story. The former occur around nexus points and generally feature some attempt to keep time lines clean (by time-traveling police charged with this duty) or to deliberately alter a time line in order to bring about preferred happenings (by time-traveling do-gooders or evildoers). The best example is Poul Anderson's Time Patrol stories. These texts foreground the primacy of events—even little-known events—in the shaping of history.

Related to the time-travel–time-policing story is the chronocracy story, which depicts a ruling body that controls time to its own advantage or to the advantage of the people it rules. Because chronocracy stories generally take place in the distant future (that is, they are a future history based on the premise that humankind has gained control of time), I do not discuss them at any length here. I label chronocracy stories as nexus stories because the ruling body alters key events, often pinpointed by a computer, in order to bring about a desired result. One example is Isaac Asimov's *The End of Eternity* (1955). In this novel, Earth is ruled by a chronocracy that carefully structures events in order to avoid loss of life, only to find that the people and culture so ruled have become stagnant. Importantly, the world in *Eternity* has lost out on space travel, implying a kind of trade-off: travel to the stars may not occur as long as a too-careful ruling body controls people and technology with the goal of preserving their lives. Stanislaw Lem notes of the chronocracy, "It is, in the end, an ineffably naive conception because no issues from philosophy or history are involved" (149). Rather, Lem argues, chronocratic rules tinker with history in order to reach some kind of equilibrium.

Texts that deal with chronocracies in religious terms include *The Fall of Chronopolis* (1974), by Barrington J. Bayley, with the Chronotic Empire ruled by a powerful Church; *Times without Number* (1969), by John Brunner, which posits a time-traveling priesthood; *Serving in Time* (1975), by Gordon Eklund; and "And Wild for to Hold" (1991), by Nancy Kress, which tells the story of an Anne Boleyn kidnapped by the Church of the Holy Hostage, a body charged with removing key figures from time and holding them hostage in order to reduce loss of life. Interestingly, most of the texts that posit chronocracies also foresee their downfall. All the texts mentioned above as examples, including *The End of Eternity*, dismantle the structure in the end, driving home the moral that history left to its own devices is more vital and useful than a history micromanaged to bring about certain outcomes for the supposed benefit of all. Just as the existence of a chronocracy in *Eternity* seemed to close off the option of space travel, the micromanaging that characterizes the chronocracy in general implies that it is self-defeating, destroying the very ends it seeks to achieve.

The last kind of nexus story, the battle story, does not focus on history and humankind's place in that matrix. Battle stories center on historically based nexus events during a war, but the focus is on military strategy and warfare for their own sakes, often without any querying of historiographic or philosophical concerns. These texts often use historical figures as characters and pay great attention to battle strategy, weapons, and warfare methods. Some examples include Harry Turtledove's *The Guns of the South* (1992), which focuses on Robert E. Lee and the Civil War, and Harry Harrison and John Holm's *The Hammer and the Cross* (1993) and its sequels. These texts— indeed, the battle story in general—depend on the Great Man theory of history, relying on the importance of certain key players to shape history. *The Hammer and the Cross*, for instance, features a strong protagonist, Shef, who makes several important technological breakthroughs that allow him to wage war effectively and to consolidate power. This single figure dramatically changes the political landscape of ninth-century Britain.

True alternate history stories take place years after a change in a nexus event, which has resulted in a radically changed world. Classic examples include Philip K. Dick's *The Man in the High Castle* (1962), Kingsley Amis's *The Alteration* (1976), and Ward Moore's *Bring the Jubilee* (1955), which is also a nexus story. These three texts take place in the "present" (the 1950s; the 1960s). In a slightly different cast is Harry Harrison's Eden trilogy, which begins with *West of Eden* (1984). This series posits humanity living in a world dominated by intelligent dinosaurs and takes place millennia ago. Brian Aldiss's *The Malacia Tapestry* (1976) also imagines a world populated by intelligent humanoid dinosaurs in a fantastic, richly textured novel that evokes a decadent Italy some time in the undetermined past. All these texts rely heavily on the notion of cause and effect. In essence, they argue that a historical event's turning out differently will in turn result in a number of other changes that cascade, culminating in worlds dramatically discontinuous with reality.

One particular kind of true alternate history is the alternate history that deals with more than just the repercussions of changed events. Texts that deal with an alternate science take the alternate history a step further and might be better called "alternate world" texts. Philip José Farmer's "Sail On! Sail On!" (1952) is one well-known example. This text initially appears to be a regular alternate history in which Roger Bacon was embraced by a Church that sponsored scientific exploration, resulting in an order of scientific religion called the Rogerians. The quirky science, which uses angel wings as a unit of measure of telegraphic wavelengths, is read as an alternative take on science, which is recast in religious terms. However, Farmer destroys our expectations—and reveals that he is writing in the alternate world genre—in the end, when we discover that the world is flat: Christopher Columbus sails off its edge. Likewise, the peculiar science expressed in this short story might then also be presumed to be true.

Similarly, Richard Garfinkle's ambitious *Celestial Matters* (1996) describes an alternate history that is also an alternate world, with a radically different scientific understanding of the world. Aristotle's conception of the universe as a series of concentric crystal spheres is literal fact, as is the music the spheres generate. Likewise, Aristotle's biology and physics are also true; for instance, doctors inject people with different sorts of humours in order to stabilize their bodies. *Celestial Matters*'s alternate history, which focuses on the Greek world engaged in a thousand-year-long war following Alexander the Great's stunning successes, is compelling, but the novel's focus is on alternate science. This novel is a novel of ideas, but it fails in its evocation of character and motivation.

Parallel worlds stories describe a number of alternate histories that exist simultaneously. Generally, protagonists can move (or at least communicate) between these parallel worlds. A good example is Frederik Pohl's *The Coming of the Quantum Cats* (1986), which features as protagonists several of the same person in different world lines. H. Beam Piper's *Lord Kalvan of*

Otherwhen (1965) and *Paratime* (1981) are other examples. In *Lord Kalvan*, a twentieth-century police officer from our world is accidentally removed to a parallel time stream, where he recreates himself as Lord Kalvan, an important ruler in a pristine new world, while the Paratime Police observe.

Parallel worlds stories assume that history can change at almost any point, no matter how apparently insignificant. All events in parallel worlds texts exist simultaneously in one time line or another. Every possible outcome of an event has occurred. Importantly, parallel worlds texts assume the importance of linear time and are less likely to imply that time is circular. Several parallel worlds stories explicitly base their premises on quantum physics.

I have organized this book according to the model of history the text best fits. After a chapter giving background on this genre, the first three text-based chapters (chapters 2, 3, and 4) all examine texts that use the genetic model of history; the last three (chapters 5, 6, and 7) each focus on one of the other three models. And whereas chapters 1 through 6 focus on alternate histories, chapter 7 focuses on alternate histories that always revert back to reality—a kind of anti–alternate history.

In chapter 1, I sketch a historical background for the alternate history as a genre. I then describe how the alternate history came to be associated with the genre of science fiction and conclude by addressing the narrative framework of the alternate history in general. This chapter provides a useful overview of the alternate history and relates it to the concerns I address throughout this book: history and narrative.

Chapter 2 discusses Ward Moore's *Bring the Jubilee*, a novel in which time does not unfold comfortably from past to present but is made to change direction. Moore seeks to recast traditional conceptions of time as it relates to history by interchanging two metaphors, time as arrow and time as cycle. By attempting to redirect the arrow of time, Moore foregrounds the malleability of historical events and the element of chance that was involved in constituting our own world. Because it queries more than one metaphor of time and change, *Bring the Jubilee* is an especially good example of the genetic paradigm of history.

Chapter 3 discusses parallel worlds texts, particularly the Paratime world in H. Beam Piper's short stories. By assuming that all worlds exist simultaneously and that several of the same individual can exist in different worlds, parallel worlds stories are concerned with the genetic model of history.

Chapter 4 discusses Philip K. Dick's *The Man in the High Castle* in historical and temporal terms. Using Paul Ricoeur's arguments about time and repetition, I argue that *High Castle* requires a rupture that disallows the use of memory. Instead, Dick relies on the individual to construct reality. This kind of construction places the individual at the center of all metaphors, for these metaphors are creations of a human mind attempting to mediate phenomenologic and cosmologic time. The world is simply a reflection of the mind. *High Castle* posits a world of randomness and overlapping spheres of influence, showing the causal relationship between people and events; it is fundamentally concerned with the genetic theory of history for this reason.

Chapter 5 discusses William Gibson and Bruce Sterling's *The Difference Engine* (1991) in terms of iteration. Gibson and Sterling use a number of narrative strategies and themes that blend the real and the unreal in novel ways. The book posits a teleological model of history, one that is concerned with final causes and the design used to get there.

Chapter 6 is a discussion of Brian Aldiss's *The Malacia Tapestry*. This novel is dramatically discontinuous with reality and is more fictive than the other texts in that the nexus event is so distant in the past and so inexplicable that it reads like fantasy. I explore the tension between history's primary metaphor of change in terms of Aldiss's refusal to address change. Instead, Aldiss relies on entropy as his main metaphor and as his model for organizing history.

In chapter 7, I discuss Poul Anderson's Time Patrol works and contrast them with true alternate histories. Though Anderson's work is persuasively historical, Anderson does not allow the alternate histories he creates to be permanent. He always destroys them and places history back on the "right" path. Anderson, a meta–alternate historian, works with the structure and nature of history. Anderson focuses on the nature of the event and the impact a single individual can have on history, and for this reason, Anderson's Time Patrol texts are deeply concerned with the causes that result in history. A brief conclusion wraps up the discussion of the texts.

Though such texts constitute a minority of alternate histories, I have decided to exclude from this study texts that rely on a reinterpretation of magic. Probably the best-known examples of such "magic works" texts are Randall Garrett's Lord Darcy books, *Murder and Magic* (1979), *Too Many Magicians* (1967), and *Lord Darcy Investigates* (1981), all of which feature Lord Darcy investigating events in a world in which magic became well understood and codified around A.D. 1300. Michael Kurland picked up Randall's thread and wrote several novels, including *Ten Little Wizards* (1988), that take place in Lord Darcy's universe. Diana Wynne Jones uses a similar nexus event in her Chrestomanci books, which begin with *The Lives of Christopher Chant* (1988). Similarly, John Whitbourne's *A Dangerous Energy* (1992) takes place in a world where magic works, although a nexus event concerning Oliver Cromwell is also dealt with. And L. E. Modesitt Jr.'s *Of Tangible Ghosts* (1994) and its sequels take place in a nicely worked out alternate world that has as one element the reality of ghosts. However, using the triumph of magic over science as a nexus event results in a fantasy text, not a science fiction text. I wish to limit myself to science fiction, as linking fantasy and historical concerns brings up a whole new set of questions.

So mainstream has the alternate history become that it is worth noting a few signs of this. First, this book is the fifth such work on this topic, the fourth in English. The three other works in English are dissertations: Edgar V. McKnight Jr.'s "Alternative History: The Development of a Literary Genre" (1994), William Joseph Collins's "Paths Not Taken: The Development, Structure, and Aesthetics of the Alternative History" (1990), and Aleksandar B. Nedelkovh's "British and American Science Fiction Novel 1950–1980 with the Theme of Alternative History (an Axiological Approach)," originally written in Serbian in 1994, with a revised and updated English edition appearing in 1999.

Collins's dissertation does what the title implies it will do; he describes the genre's development, outlines its taxonomy (the bare bones of which I outline above), and relates the genre to some well-known science fiction critics' understandings of science fiction, particularly Darko Suvin's *Metamorphoses of Science Fiction*, which Collins uses as a paradigm. He examines the alternate history as a literature of estrangement. He focuses on the historical development of the alternate history and provides excellent background for the early history of the genre, including discussions of hard-to-find early works of alternate history.

McKnight's dissertation also focuses on the alternate history's development, but he argues that it emerged as a distinct genre after World War II; thus, the primary texts McKnight engages with are more recent. McKnight also discusses science fiction literary movements such as cyberpunk (1980s) and the New Wave (1960s) and places the alternate history into this historical context.

Nedelkovich's dissertation focuses on seven science fiction texts, including Moore's *Bring the Jubilee* and Philip K. Dick's *The Man in the High Castle*. Nedelkovich's aim is to use the seven texts in order to assess the literary merit of the texts and to build criteria to aid future evaluations of alternate history texts. He also links his analyses to the sociopolitical climate of Serbia, indicating that his thinking is colored by Serbia's tendency to be anticommunist and antifascist. Nedelkovich takes as a jumping-off point Darko Suvin's notion of the novum.

There is one published dissertation in German, by Joerg Helbig, entitled *Der Parahistorische Roman. Ein Literarhistorischer und Gattungstypologischer Beitrag zur Allotopieforschung* (1987), which I have been unable to acquire and read.

The second way that we can spot the genre's move to the mainstream requires a trip to the bookstore: recent alternate histories in paperback have the words *alternate history* on the spine, indicating the recognition of the alternate history as a publishing category, a sign of the market's catering to the demands of readers. Third, mainstream writers have written alternate histories. Mystery writer Len Deighton's *SS-GB* (1978) follows a mystery case in Nazi-occupied Britain. Robert Harris's bestseller *Fatherland* (1992) is another mystery set in Nazi-occupied territory, this time Germany in 1964. *Fatherland,* a police thriller, was made into an HBO special.

Newt Gingrich, along with coauthor William R. Forstchen, has written an alternate history called *1945*. Though Gingrich is well known as a science fiction fan, he is better known as a politician, and his notoriety in this capacity has brought attention to his work as a fiction writer. And finally, several television and movie versions of alternate histories have been produced, clearly with the understanding that the sought-after audience is capable of understanding the concept of the alternate history without too much explanation. Examples include the television series *Sliders,* which has intrepid characters "sliding" from one parallel alternate world to another, sometimes meeting other versions of themselves or their companions; there are also published adventures by Brad Linaweaver based on the television program: *Sliders: The Novel* (1996) and *Sliders: Parallel Worlds* (1998). *Time Cop,* based on the movie of the same name, is a police show that has cops chasing felons through the time lanes; another relevant television series is *Quantum Leap,* which implies the possibility of alternate histories by suggesting that something in history has gone wrong and the protagonist, temporarily stuck in someone else's body, must right it to set history on its correct path. In addition to these texts are films including *Run Lola Run* (1999) and *Sliding Doors* (1998), alternate histories not marketed as such. The variety of mass culture reworkings of the alternate history show it is a viable art form that discusses the role of humanity as it creates a civilization that relies on a sense of history.

1 | Inventing the Past: A Brief Background of the Alternate History

The history of the alternate history dates to 1836, though I suspect that as scholars continue to do research, new texts will be discovered that, in retrospect, are deemed to be alternate histories. In Robert Silverberg's introduction to *Worlds of Maybe*, an anthology of alternate history stories, Silverberg mistakenly asserts that the first alternate history written was "Hands Off," by Edward Everett Hale (Silverberg, 8). The story appeared in the March 1881 issue of *Harper's* (Pinkerton, 168; Schmunk; Silverberg cites the wrong year of publication). The nexus moment of this text is Joseph's slavery in Egypt: in this text, Joseph was not sold into slavery. The narrator observes as the Phoenicians take over the Mediterranean and the world descends into barbarity. Jan Pinkerton, less given to sweeping generalizations than Silverberg, cautiously calls "Hands Off" "the first known story-length example of this genre in English or American fiction" (170)—though this is not true either. It is, however, the first example known to date of a work that deals with the time-travel paradox: a backward-traveling time traveler who causes the events he or she went back to study.

The alternate history did not exist in Western literature until 1836. This year saw the first novel-length alternate history, Louis-Napoléon Geoffroy-Chateau's *Napoléon et la conquête du monde 1812–1832, Histoire de la monarchie universelle*, better known simply as *Napoléon apocryphe*. This text follows Napoleon as he crushes all opposition and becomes emperor of the known world, finally dying in 1832. The next text of interest to students of the alternate history is Charles Renouvier's *Uchronie (L'Utopie dans l'histoire); Esquisse historique apocryphe du developpement de la civilisation européenne tel qu'il n'a pas été, tel qu'il aurait pu être*, published in 1857 and again in a revised and expanded version in 1876. Renouvier created the term *uchronie*, which is the term for the alternate history in French and which has given English the words *uchronia* and *uchronic*. Though Renouvier created the term to address "utopia in history," this sense is no longer understood, and the term is synonymous with the alternate history. The first known alternate history in English is a chapter of Isaac D'Israeli's *Curiosities of Literature* (1824) entitled "Of a History of Events which Have Not Happened."[1] Paul Alkon notes:

> Uchronias of future and alternate past history are among the modern world's most significant new ways of *imagining* human temporal relationships. Their originality is striking. . . . Before the emergence of futuristic fiction in the eighteenth century, a phenomenon most signally marked by Mercier's achievement, there was no precedent for any form allowing radical displacement of fictional time away from the present while also allowing for insistent speculative connection of the imagined time to the possible shapes of real history. ("Utopia to Uchronia," 153)

The alternate history thus filled a lack: it combined the imagined with the real. Pascal, in his *Pensées*, notes that had Cleopatra's nose been shorter, the world would have been changed. Aviezer Tucker contextualizes this: "Since Pascal, Cleopatra's nose has become the paradigmatic example of historical chaos" (276). Taming this historical chaos has become the role of the alternate history.

Several other alternate histories in English are recognized from the nineteenth century—including, of course, Mark Twain's *A Connecticut Yankee in King Arthur's Court* (1889)—and J. C. Squire's 1931 publication of *If It Had Happened Otherwise; Lapses into Imaginary History*, published in the United States as *If, or History Rewritten*, explore the realm of the alternate history with essays written by prominent and respected figures of belles lettres. Several of these essays were published in *Scribner's Magazine* in 1930 before republication in *If.* These essays speculate on what the world would be like if certain events in history had happened otherwise. The contents include Winston Churchill's "If Lee Had Not Won the Battle of Gettysburg," G. K. Chesterton's "If Don Juan of Austria Had Married Mary Queen of

Scots," and André Maurois's "If Louis XVI Had Had an Atom of Firmness." Churchill's essay cleverly reverses the idea of the alternate history by having a historian in another time stream try to imagine our history. *The Encyclopedia of Science Fiction* notes that Squire's collection was inspired by G. M. Trevelyan's essay "If Napoleon Had Won the Battle of Waterloo," published in 1907, and further notes that historians' speculations of this kind were not uncommon.

The essays in Squire's volume all display a historical sensibility and play with the generally accepted mode of creating history out of primary sources and constituting these remnants of events into a coherent story using narrative. An interesting exception, however, is Philip Guedalla's "If the Moors in Spain Had Won." This counterfactual does not tell a story but instead allows the reader to construct it by presenting information as a series of cuttings from historical texts (dutifully footnoted), travel guides, correspondence and "telegraphics," newspaper clippings, and a transcript from a session of the House of Commons. Hilaire Belloc's "If Drouet's Cart Had Stuck" uses a similar strategy. This method foregrounds the history-making process by presenting the reader with fabricated facts from "original" sources. In contrast, Winston Churchill's "If Lee Had Not Won the Battle of Gettysburg," though a depiction of a world where the South was victorious in the Civil War, is presented as a fully realized history, the product of analysis and synthesis by a scholar of history who clearly ties together cause and effect. In response to this text and two other companion pieces printed in 1930 in *Scribner's Magazine* (all three were reprinted in *If*), James Thurber wrote "If Grant Had Been Drinking at Appomattox," published in the *New Yorker* in 1930. This light short story has a drunken Grant handing over his sword to Lee when Lee comes to surrender. *If* poses questions historians and novelists cannot help but ask themselves: Who is the agent of history? Does history write itself or do others write it? What is the role of the reader in the making of history?

More recent texts that continue in the belles lettres tradition of *If* include *What If? The World's Foremost Military Historians Imagine What Might Have Been*, edited by Robert Cowley (1999); *The Hitler Options: Alternate Decisions of World War II* (1995), edited by Kenneth Macksey; *L'histoire revisitée: Panorama de l'Uchronie sous toutes ses formes* (*History Revisited: Panorama of Alternate History in Every Genre*), a book-length essay by Eric B. Henriet presenting about 500 examples of alternate histories in many genres; and *Virtual History: Alternatives and Counterfactuals*, edited by Niall Ferguson (1997). Cowley's book reprints short sidebar counterfactuals written by historians that were originally published in the spring 1998 issue of *MHQ*: *The Quarterly Journal of Military History*. In the introduction to his book, Cowley justifies the counterfactual as an acceptable method of historical inquiry by arguing: "What ifs can lead us to question long-held assumptions. What ifs can define true turning points. They can show that small accidents or split-second decisions are as likely to have major repercussions as large ones" (xi–xii).

In the field of history, alternate histories are called counterfactuals or subjunctive conditionals (Murphy, 14). The branch of history that has used counterfactuals to good effect has been economic history; particularly well known are the applied economics counterfactual analyses of "the railroad, slavery, and British industrial growth" (Murphy, 33).[2] This overwhelmingly American branch of history making, also known as cliometrics, relies heavily on statistical analyses of various kinds of data. Cliometricians "are defined by a methodology rather than by any particular subject-matter or interpretation of the nature of historical change" (Stone, 6).

Unsurprisingly, counterfactuals have been attacked by historians because they are untrue. Perhaps the most famous remark a historian has made about the alternate history is that of E. H. Carr, who called the counterfactual an "idle parlor game" (Cowley, xi). George G. S. Murphy, however, argues they should be used, in part because they are useful and in part because "the demand that we deprive historical language of 'fictions' can have quite undesirable consequences. If we define a 'fiction' as a statement to which we cannot assign a definite value 'true,' very little is left in human discourse" (Murphy, 28).

Murphy's focus on the notion of truth actually gets to the heart of the problem historians have with counterfactuals: with so much work to be done in finding and writing the truth, why bother with something patently false? However, counterfactuals have a very real use in the field of history: they foreground the notion of cause and effect that is so important to historians when they construct a narrative. Steven Weber believes that counterfactuals are important because they "can also be used to open minds, to raise tough questions about what we think we know, and to suggest unfamiliar or uncomfortable arguments that we had best consider" (Weber, 268). Johannes Bulhof says of counterfactuals: "They help identify causes, and hence help explain events in history. They are used to defend judgments about people, and to highlight the importance of particular events" (145). Bulhof goes on to argue persuasively that counterfactuals are valuable because they justify the importance of events. They allow the historian to make inferences and draw conclusions. Using a variety of examples from everyday (that is, noncounterfactual) historical writings, Bulhof shows how historians have used counterfactual assertions explicitly or implicitly to highlight the importance of their assertions — their explanation of why something happened. For instance, a historian may say in passing something like, "If the letter had not been misdirected, things would have turned out quite differently." This throws open the possibility that something else could possibly have happened, even if it did not, and it also foregrounds the importance of the event in the chain of cause and effect. In order to assert that a historical event was important, a historian must have the ability to see the other side: that it could have happened differently. Thus, the most common use of counterfactuals in historical discourse is to highlight the importance of events (Bulhof, 151–52). Possibly the best-known example of a historian's use of a counterfactual is Robert William Fogel's work on the the role of the railroads in the economic growth of the United States, summarized in his *Railroads and American Economic Growth; Essays in Econometric History* (1964). Using data from the time, Fogel constructed a math-based model based on the assumption that the United States had not developed a railroad system. He concluded that not much would have been different.

Although one criticism of the counterfactual by historians is that they are frivolous and untrue, the recent books of collected essays that focus on counterfactuals attempt to reign the genre in — to limit its scope and thereby make it respectable (and to further differentiate it from the fictive works that are the subject of this book). Niall Ferguson, in his introduction to the edited volume *Virtual History*, after giving a quick rundown of examples of the alternate history from mass-culture artifacts such as films, tosses off, "Of course, Hollywood and science fiction are not academically respectable" (3). Ferguson distances himself from mass-culture artifacts by speaking of counterfactuals' need for plausibility; he notes that the essays in *Virtual History* "are not mere fantasy: they are simulations based on calculations about the relative probability of plausible outcomes in a chaotic world" (Ferguson, 85). Robert Cowley decries counterfactuals that are outside the realm of reasonable possibility as "frivolous": he notes that when gathering the texts that make up *What If?* he avoided implausible scenarios, such as Hannibal possessing an H-bomb (xiii). Similarly, Kenneth Macksey, editor of a volume of counterfactuals about World War II, notes in his prologue that the authors were asked to "[keep] within the bounds of credibility and reality and [project] ideas based on actual situations. People behave normally, in character. The appearance of later technology is avoided" (12). Such limitations are a reasonable way to limit the scope of a book of collected works; these limitations also provide a useful departure point for alternate histories, which can feel free to step outside the bounds of credulity.

The importance of the counterfactual to historians might be summed up as follows. When a scientist runs an experiment, she is able to control for variables. In fact, the hallmark of a well-run experiment is its reproducibility. Narratively, this is expressed in scientific discourse by a scholarly article's materials and methods section, which is designed to provide all the details of an experiment to anyone who might care to reproduce it. But in history, it is not possible to control for these variables; not only are there too many of them, but the historian lacks the power to isolate some and experiment with others. Counterfactuals allow the historian to run an experiment when the system is too complex (as history): the historian can hold everything else consistent and change one thing. Robert Jervis notes that "counterfactuals show the limits of our standard comparative method and make us look for the hidden connections that tie the system together" (Jervis, 313). But more than just "hidden connections" may be queried. Aviezer Tucker notes that the counterfactual can be important because it helps the historian figure out how important a particular cause was in bringing about the effect being studied: Counterfactuals may be constructed that "isolate the effects of each cause separately, and then compar[e] them with the actual historical result. The greater the difference, the more important the cause" (Tucker, 266). Counterfactuals are thus useful for historians, and I argue that the fictive versions of counterfactuals, as expressed in genre science fiction writing, maintain their importance in terms of querying cause and effect usefully.

Though the alternate history began as a literature concerned with social commentary, as were the texts by Geoffroy-Chateau and Renouvier, the genre quickly combined with historians' counterfactuals. This allowed authors to combine elements of the history with elements of novelistic technique in their texts. The first science fiction treatment of alternate worlds is generally recognized as Murray Leinster's 1934 "Sidewise in Time," published in *Amazing Stories*, the leading science fiction magazine of the time. This text introduced the "what if history took a different turn" story to genre science fiction. The story focuses on a bizarre natural upheaval of possible time lines and the group of characters that traverses them. This story does not construct and sustain a single well-developed alternate world but instead shows several possible worlds as characters from our world stumble from time line to time line.

The first science fiction story to develop and sustain an alternate world is L. Sprague De Camp's *Lest Darkness Fall* (1941), in which a lightning strike sends historian Martin Padway back in time to sixth-century Italy. Realizing he is at a crucial juncture of history, he decides to do what he can to keep the Roman Empire from falling, thus keeping five centuries of the Dark Ages at bay. He succeeds in changing history, but the real interest of the story lies in Padway's ingenuity and in the well-drawn world of Italy in A.D. 535. Since then, countless alternate histories have been published, most inside (but some outside) the genre—so many that, as I mention in the introduction, the field has become a publishing category.

Though much work has been done linking history and fiction together via narrative, the primary fiction texts used for discussion tend to be classics. For instance, both Erich Auerbach, in *Mimesis*, and Dominick LaCapra, in *History, Politics, and the Novel*, discuss Stendhal's *Le Rouge et Le Noir* (*Red and Black*) and Woolf's *To the Lighthouse*. Certain texts (particularly Woolf's), because of their relationship to truth, reality, and subjectivity—and because of their undisputed greatness—get written about. In addition, writing about fictive texts that are continuous with reality makes sense, as these texts foreground the similarities between fiction and history. Auerbach notes that the genre of the novel has tended to embrace realism, including novels that featured common characters rather than the elite: "Realism had to embrace the whole reality of contemporary civilization, in which to be sure the bourgeoisie played a dominant role, but in which the masses were beginning to press threateningly ahead as they became ever more conscious of their own function and power" (497). As a genre, the novel should tell us about our world and should use as its protagonists people from all classes.

The role of fantastic literature in relationship to historical and narrative analyses has not been dealt with extensively. I chose to use historical analysis in this study of the alternate history because the alternate history is the branch of science fiction that deals most directly with historical analysis. The practical reason that the alternate history is classified as science fiction is simply that the authors of alternate histories tend to be established science fiction writers. (There are, of course, numerous exceptions.) These works are thus classified and shelved with science fiction, because the writer has already been categorized as a science fiction writer. In the introduction, I point out why the alternate history should be classified as science fiction.

Several aspects of history link it with fiction. Among them is the notion of reenactment (Collingwood). Historical writing seeks to re-create a historical milieu, and realistic fiction seeks to reenact a milieu that accurately refers to reality. In addition, the historian and the fiction writer build their texts out of traces of the past, such as documents or other physical remains. The fictive element of history links the historian and the fiction writer. The historian, like the fiction writer, ultimately decides what kind of story is told. Of course, as fiction, the alternate history tends to focus on the role of the individual and his or her role in shaping history (a variation of the Great Man theory of history, which holds that individuals, rather than social forces, shape history).

The aspect of history that most closely links it with science fiction is its status as Other. Ricoeur, following White, argues that history, with its temporal distance from the present, "tends as a whole to *make the past remote* from the present" (Ricoeur, *Reality*, 15; Ricoeur's emphasis). Ricoeur goes on to argue that to make this remote past comprehensible to the contemporary reader, the historian must prefigure his or her narrative; again following White, Ricoeur believes such prefiguration is tropological—that is, figurative. Ricoeur notes:

> We must therefore not confuse the *iconic* value of representation of the past with a model, in the sense of a scale model, like a geographical map, for there is no original given with which to compare the model. It is precisely the strangeness of the original, as the documents make it appear, that gives rise to the effort of history to prefigure the style proper to it. This is why there is no metaphorical relation between a narrative and a course of events: The reader is directed toward a sort of figure that likens the events reported to a narrative form with which our culture has made us familiar. (Ricoeur, *Reality*, 32)

Constituting a narrative through conscious or unconscious tropological choices is therefore an attempt to make the past explicable to a modern reader through culturally determined narrative choices.

The role of narrative in history has been the subject of much debate among historiographers. There is no question that history is assembled by language, and White's influential and controversial writings have shown us that the historian is complicitous in the construction of history. The historian can no longer be thought of as an outsider looking in but must be thought of instead as a participant. (Unsurprisingly, alternate histories that deal with time travel play with the notion of historian as participant. Ward Moore's *Bring the Jubilee* does this literally as a historian travels in time to the site of a Civil War battle and changes its outcome.) Even R. G. Collingwood, an influential, classic-minded historian whose writings are held up by contemporary critics so that they might work against them, admits that historians are participants in the stories they tell. Collingwood goes so far as to say: "As works of imagination, the historian's work and the novelist's do not differ. Where they do differ is that the historian's picture is meant to be true" (246).

The brief but important rise of the *Annales* school to the fore of cutting-edge historical criticism is an example of the field of history's attempts to move outside Rankean narrative, only to return to it when a new critical sensibility made itself manifest. The *Annales* school, named after an important journal, was cofounded by Lucien Febvre and Marc Bloch (Ricoeur, *Time and Narrative*, 1:102). Historians such as Fernand Braudel (*The Mediterranean and the Mediterranean World in the Age of Philip II* [1949, 1966]) wrote works cleaving to its unorthodox style. Ricoeur describes the purpose of the *Annales* moment in historiographic thought:

> In fact, what the founders of the Annales school had wanted to fight against in the first place was fascination with the unique, unrepeatable event, then the identification of history with an improved chronology of the state, and finally—and perhaps above all—the absence of a criterion of choice, and therefore of any problem, in the elaboration of what counts as a "fact" in history. The facts . . . are not given in the documents, rather documents are selected as a function of certain problems. (*Time and Narrative*, 1:107–8)

Hans Kellner notes that one important aspect of the *Annales* school was its lack of emphasis on "discrete human events" (8). The *Annales* school's benefit was that it attempted to circumvent narrative, using in its place collections of facts or other unorthodox collections from which meaning can be derived.

Braudel, in his preface to the first edition of *Mediterranean*, notes that he wrote the book as he did—that is, eschewing a typical narrative structure—because "the historical narrative is not a method, or even the objective method *par excellence*, but quite simply a philosophy of history like any other" (21). This long work, twice revised and a triumph of scholarship, has as its aim an examination of history on a number of levels: timeless history, which discusses the physical land (chapter 1 is called "The Peninsulas: Mountains, Plateaux, and Plains"; Braudel notes he wishes to "explore . . . all the permanent, slow-moving, or recurrent features of Mediterranean life" in the first part of the book [353]); the history of groups and related elements such as economic systems; and the history of individual people and events. Braudel provides a view of every conceivable aspect of the region through exhaustive discussions, dutifully footnoted, that range through a number of vantage points. He does not organize *Mediterranean* around a single, tightly controlled thesis; the book does not even focus on Philip II. Braudel seeks range and scope.

Though the preface to the first edition places the work in a historical moment and relates it to critical notions current at the time, in the preface to the second edition, Braudel backpedals. He speaks of the "dazzling early period of the *Annales* of Marc Bloch and Lucien Febvre," but then goes on to say that "they are attacks on old positions, forgotten in the research world, if not in the teaching world of today, yesterday's polemic chasing shadows from the past" (15). When narrative began to be problematized again (that is, when White brought the question of narrative back to the fore), the *Annales* school was supplanted by a new critical trend.

When historians deal with literature and the literature–history link— and they do—what sorts of works do they choose to study? Stephen Bann believes that those useful to examine are those that work on "comparing and collating different models of time and history, while placing in suspension traditional devices for signalling the opposition between fact and fiction. . . . The difficulty is precisely one of making concrete the mythic structures which govern our apprehension of time, and displaying them not as a precondition of the text but as emerging from the text" (Bann, *Inventions*, 74).[3] By exploring time and history, Bann foregrounds the mythic nature so expressed. Paul Ricoeur believes that fiction of interest is a text in which "the very experience of time" is "at stake in these structural transformations"; he believes texts such as Virginia Woolf's *Mrs. Dalloway*, Marcel Proust's *A la recherche du temps perdu*, and Thomas Mann's *Der Zauberberg* (*The Magic Mountain*) are "tales about time," a notion he borrows from A. A. Mendilow (Ricoeur, *Time and Narrative*, 2:101), which is the kind of fictive work he believes is worth studying with historical concerns in mind. The alternate history is the rare form of literature that tells tales about time. The goal of the alternate history is to bring to the fore historical and temporal concerns. The alternate history directly addresses the concerns of history and the concerns of cause and effect on events.

The term *narrative* must be one of those words that everybody knows because only rarely is the term defined. Even when defined, the words *narrative, story,* and *plot* are used synonymously. A striking number of definitions I have run across use the word being defined in the definition. For instance, the first definition of narrative in *Webster's Tenth* is simply "something that is narrated" or "story." The third definition is of more help: "the representation in art of an event or story." Tellingly, the word *narrate* has as a root a Latin word for "to know." In general, it is understood that a narrative is a telling of a story that can be linked into a system of cause and effect by ordering time, though the work of art in question need not be expressed chronologically.

Where narrative comes from seems to be its own question and is not one of my concerns in this discussion; the general feeling of many critics, including Roland Barthes and Paul Ricoeur, is that narrative just is—it is universal. Barthes says that "narrative is international, transhistorical, transcultural: it is simply there, like life itself" (79). Likewise, why we use narrative so frequently is a bone of contention. Many critics argue that narrative is a way to structure reality. Others argue that narrative constitutes reality. Others, including Martin Heidegger and Hans-Georg Gadamer, argue "that every description of reality is an interpretation, a product of our historically conditioned concepts and values" (McCullagh, 232). Some critics attempt to divorce the role of narrative from the constitution of reality: Paul Ricoeur sees narrative as a kind of metaphor. (Indeed, *Time and Narrative* was designed to be a companion to his earlier book, *The Rule of Metaphor.*) For Ricoeur, narrative does not describe reality but "the privileged means by which we re-configure our confused, unformed, and at the limit mute temporal experience" (*Time and Narrative,* 1:xi). Narrative's ubiquitousness is one reason Barthes links it to the state of being human. Fredric Jameson believes that analysis of narratives may reveal "the outlines of some deeper and vaster narrative moment in which the groups of a given collectivity at a certain historical conjuncture anxiously interrogate their fate" (148), implying that narrative is a strategy used by individuals to make sense of life. David Carr feels that narrative is socially constructed and not universal or somehow basic to the human condition. Carr sees narrative as something that constitutes action rather than something that redescribes action (51).

I summarize these points about narrative and its function and role to show how richly this topic has been problematized by critics. But with the question of narrative and its purpose and origins aside, just what is narrative? Lawrence Stone defines narrative as "the organization of material in a chronologically sequential order and the focusing of the content into a single coherent story, albeit with sub-plots" (3). F. R. Ankersmit, in a discussion of historical narrative, does not define the term *narrative*, instead using the related term *narratio* to mean "the historiographical, narrative representation of the past" from a particular point of view, presumably that of the historian/writer (12, 19), thus emphasizing the subject-object nature of historical narrative and the importance of point of view when writing a narrative. Ankersmit thus prefers to coin a new word to discuss his concept rather than use the already established word *narrative* in order that his meaning might be distinct. Historian Nancy Partner plays up narrative as a tool used in both fiction and history by noting that "the central conventions which govern all narrative—the organization of time, the distinction between contingent and significant sequence, alias story—unite history and fiction profoundly and permanently" ("Making Up," 96). This definition is useful because it foregrounds the elements that make up narrative while stressing the notion of cause and effect.

Behind all definitions and analyses of narrative is the notion of narrative as story: a series of temporal events linked by cause and effect. The alternate history sheds light on the notion of cause and effect by focusing on events that occurred differently, thus foregrounding the notion of cause and effect (not to mention chance). Of course, many literary genres foreground cause and effect: Biographies assume that what happened in the past resulted in the subject under discussion. The whole idea of a biography is predicated upon the notion that events in the past affect the present. Mysteries lay out cause and effect around the dinner table over drinks, just as the detective utters the words, "You may be wondering why I have brought you all together." Science fiction also foregrounds cause and effect with its "if this goes on" message.

What about the notion of *cause and effect* itself? I am not using the term in any specialized way. C. Behan McCullagh defines cause and effect as follows, a definition I cite because of its clarity:

Historians judge one event or state of affairs to have been a cause of another, I suggest, only if they believe the occurrence of the first to have been necessary in the circumstances, contingently necessary, for the occurrence of the second. . . . Roughly speaking, one event or state of affairs is a cause of another if, had the former been different in some way and everything else remained the same, the latter would not have occurred as it did. In that sense we can say that the occurrence of the first was necessary in the circumstances for the occurrence of the second, and therefore a cause of it. (176)

No surprises here. In the field of history, McCullagh goes on to note, one way to study the notion of cause and effect (to determine if events are really linked or to study the significance of cause) is to construct a counterfactual. One may then examine the counterfactual and the real and analyze the two to come to some conclusion about the cause.

Narrativity, with its reliance on cause and effect, is characterized by its temporal nature. Ricoeur links narrativity and temporality with circular reasoning: "I take temporality to be that structure of existence that reaches language in narrativity and narrativity to be the language structure that has temporality as its ultimate referent" ("Narrative Time," 169). David Wood argues that in narrative, there are six kinds of temporality: "that of the reader, the narrator, the plot, the action, the characters, and of the narrative discourse itself" (8). Frank Kermode discusses the temporal nature of narrative and of plot by using the metaphor of a clock ticking, noting that "the interval between *tock* and *tick* represents purely successive, disorganized time of the sort that we need to humanize . . . the interval must be purged of simple chronicity, of the emptiness of *tock-tick*, humanly uninteresting successiveness" (45–46). The solution—the element that gives meaning to the empty successiveness of *tick* and *tock* (and it is no accident that a device that measures time is used as the metaphor here)—is "'temporal integration'—our way of bundling together perception of the present, memory of the past, and expectation of the future, in a common organization" (46). This divides chronology into notions such as past, present, and future.

One of the most significant scholars of the role of narrative in historiography is Hayden White, whose *Metahistory: The Historical Imagination in Nineteenth-Century Europe* shook the historical world, because he suggested that the writings of historians are constructed to tell a story (via narrative) and that the historian is complicitous in this storytelling, not an objective, impartial recorder of events. In this formalist analysis, White argues that historians arrange their works using four tropes: metaphor, metonymy, synecdoche, and irony. His introduction declares that his aim is to "consider the historical work as what it most manifestly is—that is to say, a verbal structure in the form of a narrative prose discourse that purports to be a model, or icon, of past structures and processes in the interest of *explaining what they were by representing* them" (*Metahistory*, 2; White's emphasis). White upset the historical world by suggesting in *Metahistory* that the historian invents elements that allow the story to hang together (White, 6–7); obviously, this calls into question the historian's ability to act as a disinterested, totally objective scholar. This position contrasts with that of Collingwood, who argues that the historian makes reasoned, intelligent inferences from information found in historically correct sources.[4] White brings together history and fiction by suggesting that they can be created and analyzed using the same techniques.

Likewise, Paul Ricoeur has done much work in this field, with equally far-ranging results. In *Time and Narrative*, he concludes that "the actual interweaving of fiction and history occurs in the refiguration of time" (3:185). Whereas White tends to see narrativity linking with tropological concerns to tell a story, Ricoeur sees narrativity linking with temporality. Narrative is so ingrained in humanity, Ricoeur believes, that it is impossible to get beyond it; for this reason, "there can be no thought about time without narrated time" (3:241).

Ricoeur speaks directly to the questions I pose: How and where do history and fiction meet? For Ricoeur, narrated time mediates between phenomenologic time (that is, time as experienced) and cosmologic time (that is, time as expressed by the earth's rotation and circuit around the sun, which we measure using clocks and calendars) (3:243–44). The alternate history expresses this and other ideas by using metaphors of time such as time as cycle and time as arrow, which I discuss in chapter 2.

Texts that concern themselves with history rely on several well-established notions of history. As I mentioned in the introduction, there are four broad models of history, each implying that history has a different aim. These are the eschatological, genetic, entropic, and teleological models of history. These constructions are firmly ingrained in our conceptions of history and time. History relies on the notion that the past and the present are separate but related things, a notion based in turn on our personal experience: a past leads to a now (a moment we cannot escape from) and, presumably, to a future. This is the linear conception of time — the conception of time's arrow, and it implies the genetic model of history, which is concerned with causal antecedents.

I borrow the terms *time's arrow* and its attendant term *time's cycle* in part from Stephen Jay Gould, whose 1987 *Time's Arrow, Time's Cycle* examines these metaphors in some detail. Gould notes that conceptions of time have revolved around these two metaphors, each with a different purpose. Time's arrow implies that "history is an irreversible sequence of unrepeatable events," with "linked events moving in a direction" (10–11). When historians constitute events into language—that is, when they write history—they tie together events using cause and effect, often structuring the events from exposition to rising action to climax to denouement, as fiction is written.

White argues that "the historian arranges the events in the chronicle into a hierarchy of significance by assigning events different functions as story elements in such a way as to disclose the formal coherence of a whole set of events considered as a comprehensible process with a discernible beginning, middle, and end" (*Metahistory*, 7). Like fiction, history requires imagination and invention on the part of the writer. In any case, patterning a piece of writing into beginning, middle, and end presupposes the primacy of time's arrow.

Unsurprisingly, alternate histories that focus on time travel or the "crucial event" (which I call the "nexus event") make use of history and what history purports to do. We need history not only to understand the changes the alternate historian has added; we also need to study history in order to see how alternate historians structure their works, as alternate historians use some of the same strategies and methods as historians. R. G. Collingwood, summing up the traditional meaning and object of history, classifies history as a science, a form "of thought whereby we ask questions and try to answer them" (9). History studies *res gestae* (things done), or actions that have occurred in the past. Historians then interpret this information. The end is "human self-knowledge" (10). Collingwood reinforces the belief that historians concern themselves with knowable events, or facts, by use of the document or trace.

In *Metahistory*, White rethinks this traditional approach, discarding the notion that historians can be objective. He argues that the difference perceived between writing history and writing fiction is not as great as historians would have us believe:

It is sometimes said that the aim of the historian is to explain the past by "finding," "identifying," or "uncovering" the "stories" that lie buried in chronicles; and that the difference between "history" and "fiction" resides in the fact that the historian "finds" his stories, whereas the fiction writer "invents" his. This conception of the historian's task, however, obscures the extent to which "invention" also plays a part in the historian's operations. (White, *Metahistory*, 6–7)

White argues in *Metahistory* that creating history involves the same strategies as creating fictive narratives, and that like fictive narratives, historical writings need to be analyzed tropologically.

But implicit in White's argument, as in the alternate history's conceptions of history, is the thought that the past and present are different but related, since events in the past have made the present what it is today. One way to bridge the gap between past and present is to travel from the present to the past—to be there. Naturally, historians find this impossible, but I suspect a historian would leap at the chance to go back in time and see a crucial event firsthand. This very desire leads to the climax of Ward Moore's alternate history *Bring the Jubilee*, where a historian travels back in time to visit the site of the decisive battle that led the South to win the Civil War. He discovers, however, that it is all too easy to change the course of events, and his inadvertent meddling wipes out his history.

Alternate histories capitalize on this desire to know firsthand. They are one way of rewriting history: the author uses a combination of real history and invention seamlessly combined. Alternate historians use the same strategies as both writers and historians: they take a historical base, accurate in our world, synthesized from eyewitness accounts, letters, and other primary sources, and historical repercussions of the event (war, peace, an important treaty, lands exchanged, and so on) and add fictional characters and events to it. The difference between the reality of the event and the alternate history creates tension that keeps the reader interested. The writer tells the story in narrative form and uses the narrative techniques that fiction and history share.

The alternate history differs fundamentally from historical fiction, however, although they have several similarities. Historical novels attempt to create as realistically as possible the past's milieu. Alternate histories, of course, often do the same. However, historical novels are peopled with characters who are part of the past milieu. In alternate histories, this may also be the case, but it is just as likely that a time traveler, of a different milieu, may be experiencing the past as an outsider. The fundamental difference is that of historical inquiry. Historical novels seek to uphold the events of history as they occurred—to tell the truth. By their very definition, alternate histories must change the historical event. Historical novels uphold the "true" version of history, whereas the alternate history dismantles it. In an alternate history, an event must change. Naturally, in a historical novel, the writer will, for the sake of the story, create characters or events that did not occur—for instance, the writer might invent a servant that Mary, Queen of Scots never had. (This is, of course, why historical novels are novels and not meant to be biographies or true histories.) However, in a historical novel, the end of the story must be as events have specified: Mary, Queen of Scots must be beheaded. If she overthrows Elizabeth and becomes ruler of England and Scotland, then the text becomes an alternate history: it has challenged the events in question by changing them. Hayden White, in *Metahistory,* remarks on the difference between literary fictions and historical works:

> Unlike literary fictions, such as the novel, historical works are made up of events that exist outside the consciousness of the writer. The events reported in a novel can be invented in a way that they cannot be (or are not supposed to be) in a history. . . . Unlike the novelist, the historian confronts a veritable chaos of events *already constituted,* out of which he must choose the elements of the story he would tell. (*Metahistory,* 6n; White's emphasis)

Alternate historians embellish what is "already constituted" with new characters, but they must also include the changed event that causes the problem of the alternate history story. The author tells the story in narrative form and uses the narrative techniques that fiction and history share. Alternate histories combine a historian's strategies with a fiction writer's strategies, often so successfully that readers find themselves hard pressed to tell where one ends and the other begins.

The link between cause and effect is always an interpretation made by the person looking. In history, the effect will be the event expressed through the trace—the battle, the treaty, the marriage, all recorded by contemporaries. The historian will construct a reason for the effect, one grounded in letters, tax rolls, legal decisions, and other traces. This reason will be her argument, the thesis of her work. But in history, the leap between cause and effect will always be an interpretation. In fiction (and of course in the alternate history), the connection between cause and effect is not an interpretation but an invention. The space between the narratively structured *tock* and *tick* (to borrow Kermode's clock) is filled with meaning, the theme of the work, which allows the readers to organize the past, present, and future of the text. In the alternate history, this organization occurs by comparing the text with what is known—with reality—and holding it up alongside the narrative of the text itself. The interpretation we expect when we read of the historical events crucial to a nexus event will not occur, so the notion of cause and effect is in play until the author decides to fill us in by telling us the point of historical departure. In alternate history texts, the "temporal integration" that Kermode speaks of is turned on its head, because "memory of the past," in its strictest sense, will not work. Cause and effect has been disrupted. There is, of course, the memory of the past events that occurred in the text under discussion. Whereas history and historical fiction explain the world as it is or was, the alternate history explains the world as it might be, as it could have been, or even as it should have been.

Poul Anderson's Time Patrol works, discussed at length in chapter 7, are a good example of history making mixed with story making. Anderson sets his Time Patrol works in our history; his stories often focus around a key historical event, such as the Second Punic War, that Time Patrol members must preserve. Because of their overtly historical slant, these stories deal with the nature of history and historical inquiry. All the Time Patrol stories have at their heart an event that goes wrong. Some Time Patrol member, often the heroic, pipe-smoking Manse Everard, must set that event right again, thus putting history back on the proper track. Anderson's works are also interesting because the nexus event is often not an obvious or well-known one. Anderson discards the popular nexus events of World War II or the Civil War in favor of little-known events, thus implying that these dimly remembered past events have had civilization-defining significance.

The remarks about history making I have made thus far are particularly suited to alternate histories that deal with time travel and that focus on particularly important nexus events (for instance, a battle), where the writer combines what is real with what is invented. Stories that move further away from the event and deal with the event's repercussions, such as Kingsley Amis's *The Alteration* (1976), feel more fictive than factual because they depict ordinary people living out ordinary lives in bizarre worlds. This kind of text is not set in a past we recognize but a "present" we do not.

Interestingly, a surprising number of alternate histories, including *Alteration*, have alternate history texts mentioned within them. The alternate history within an alternate history serves two purposes, besides the obvious one of a bit of metahumor: it causes the reader to hold up his or her world against that of the alternate world, as the alternate history alluded to may be that of the reader (it rarely is, but we always hope); and it focuses the reader's attention on key questions the writer is focusing on in his or her text. The best example of the latter purpose is *The Grasshopper Lies Heavy*, the banned alternate history mentioned in Philip K. Dick's

The Man in the High Castle (1962). *Grasshopper* presumes that the Allied powers won World War II, though the world detailed in *Grasshopper* is not quite our world. *Grasshopper* was created by chance, as the author used a divining technique to write the book for him. Dick makes the point that the world was created by chance and by individual consciousness. Amis alludes to *Grasshopper* and *High Castle* in his own fictive banned alternate history, making a bow to Dick and foregrounding the oppressiveness of the Catholic power structure.

Because *Alteration* takes place in the 1970s, centuries after the nexus event (Luther does not split from the Catholic Church and becomes pope), the world does not seem based on recognized historical events, as do Anderson's texts set in the past, but science fictional. Amis creates a world markedly different from the one we expect, but his inquiry is still historical, based on a cause-and-effect theory of history. Alternate histories are the ideal texts to analyze in terms of temporality because they deal with disruptions in history and time.

2 | Ward Moore's *Bring the Jubilee:* Alternate History, Narrativity, and the Nature of Time

In this chapter, I discuss in detail several articulations of time, most notably the ideas of time as an arrow and time as a cycle. Underpinning any understanding of time, however, is the human sense of time and the way it is structured. History is held up by this most basic of understandings: what happened in the past has created the present. The alternate history seeks to redirect the arrow of time, to change a cause and therefore change an effect, an idea I outlined in more detail in the previous chapter. In an alternate history, even a simple change in cause may cascade, leading to a dramatically different effect, or historical outcome. For this reason, I consider all alternate histories to be fundamentally genetic, or, to cite *Webster's Tenth*, "relating to or determined by the origin, development or causal antecedents of something." This chapter and the two that follow focus on texts that deal primarily with the genetic model of history.

Bring the Jubilee, Ward Moore's classic 1955 science fiction novel, plays with the genesis of events by playing with the metaphors we use to articulate the passage of time, most notably the metaphors of time as arrow and time as cycle—the linear and cyclic models of time. I discuss these metaphors in terms of both the theme of the work and the narrative structure Moore uses: Moore writes the memoir of a historian, Hodge, who finds himself in an increasingly alien alternate reality after he time-travels to the past and changes his history. Hodge, who fears that he lives in a world of endlessly repeating elements, accidentally redirects the arrow of time when he travels to an important battle site and wipes out the history of himself and of all those he loves.

Jubilee is a true alternate history, or one that shows the repercussions of changed events years or centuries after the event has occurred; usually, the characters are unaware they live in the "wrong" history. This genre of the alternate history has produced some real classics. The Nazis' winning World War II is one popular topic: Philip K. Dick's *The Man in the High Castle* (1962), the subject of chapter 4, is perhaps the best known, but other novels on the topic include Brad Linaweaver's *Moon of Ice* (1988), in which the Nazis get the atomic bomb; Stephen Fry's delightfully funny *Making History* (1996), which argues that maybe Hitler wasn't so bad, compared to what might have been; *SS-GB: Nazi-Occupied Britain 1941* (1978), a police procedural by mystery writer Len Deighton; Sarban's *The Sound of His Horn* (1952), about a man who enters his future, in which Germany won World War II; and Robert Harris's *Fatherland* (1992), which takes place in 1964 Nazi Berlin. Other well-known true alternate histories include John Brunner's *Times without Number* (1969), Keith Roberts's *Pavane* (1966), and Phyllis Eisenstein's *Shadow of Earth* (1979); the first two describe worlds in which the Spanish conquered England, and the last one describes an America ruled by Spanish conquerers. Kingsley Amis's *The Alteration* (1976) deals with a 1970s world in which the Roman Catholic Church was never rocked by Protestantism. Harry Harrison's *Tunnel through the Deeps* (1972), also published under the title *A Transatlantic Tunnel, Hurrah!*, has a descendant of the executed traitor George Washington, in a world in which the American Revolution failed, build a transatlantic tunnel. *The Difference Engine* (1991), by William Gibson and Bruce Sterling, posits a world in which the computer age occurred during the reign of Queen Victoria; this text is the subject of chapter 5. Norman Spinrad's *The Iron Dream* (1972) tells us about Adolf Hitler, award-winning science fiction writer. And the Nova African characters in Terry Bisson's utopian *Fire on the Mountain* (1988) get ready to land on Mars about a hundred years after John Brown's successful raid on Harper's Ferry.

In addition to texts that take place years after the nexus event has resulted in a different reality, many texts focus on the nexus event itself, often a battle, and we watch as it goes "wrong." Poul Anderson's Time Patrol stories play with nexus events, as I outline in chapter 7. Harry Harrison's *Rebel in Time* (1983) and Harry Turtledove's *The Guns of the South*

(1992) tell of the attempts of time travelers to alter the outcome of the Civil War in order to ensure that the South will win and slavery will continue. Kevin J. Anderson and Doug Beason's *The Trinity Paradox* (1991) throws an environmentalist back in time to 1943, where she is given the opportunity to sabotage the Trinity atom bomb test, allowing the Nazis to develop the atomic bomb first. These and other nexus stories rely on time travel, allowing someone with knowledge of history to pinpoint an event and attempt to sabotage it. By controlling cause, these texts tell us, one can control effect.

Jubilee, by dint of time-travel usage near the end of the novel, is both a true alternate history and a nexus story. The novel begins as a true alternate history in a world where the South won the Civil War, then becomes a nexus alternate history focusing on the Battle of Gettysburg when the protagonist travels back in time to study this battle. Because of its use of time travel, the novel questions the connection between history and its assumptions about chronology. *Jubilee* queries the two most fundamental time metaphors, time as arrow and time as cycle, by collapsing them.

Hodge Backmaker, the protagonist of *Bring the Jubilee,*[1] writes of his study to become a historian:

> I also began to understand the central mystery of historical theory. When and what and how and where, but the when is the least. Not chronology but relationship is ultimately what the historian deals in. The element of time, so vital at first glance, assumes a constantly more subordinate character. That the past is past becomes ever less important. Except for perspective it might as well be the present or the future or, if one can conceive it, a parallel time. I was not investigating a petrification but a fluid. (137–38)

Jubilee seeks to explore "the element of time" that Hodge ponders in this passage. His words are prescient: he discovers firsthand that the past "might as well be the present or the future." In this novel, time does not unfold comfortably from past to present but is made to change direction. Moore seeks to recast traditional conceptions of time as it relates to history. The very fact that one can posit a "history" that never happened implies the changeability of history and the element of chance that was involved in constituting our own world.

The novel opens in the United States of the 1930s—but in the twenty-six United States after their defeat by the Confederates in the War of Southron

Independence, what we would call the Civil War. This text, and indeed alternate histories in general, query such interests as the nature of time, the role of the individual in history, and the impact of nexus events on the texture of everyday reality. One of the key concepts in alternate history texts is the doubt they cast on the inevitability of the here and now by showing the results of the alteration of one historical change, whether large (a decisive battle during the Civil War affecting hundreds of soldiers, as in *Jubilee*) or small (a small boy fails to pick up a magnet while playing one day). The intimate details in *Jubilee* that tell of everyday life in the altered continuum validate the alternate history while simultaneously raising doubts in the reader's mind about what is taken for granted.

Also important to alternate histories is the differentiation between what Hegel calls "original history" and "reflective history." Firsthand accounts make up original history, written by "the class of historians who have themselves witnessed, experienced and lived through the deeds, events and situations they describe, who have themselves participated in these events and in the spirit which informed them" (Hegel, 12). Original historians describe not the past but the present; it is this desire to see events firsthand that provides the impetus of alternate histories that use time travel. On the other hand, historians engaging in creating reflective history are of another consciousness than the age they study. The past and present are now separate, but, as Hegel says, "the writer approaches it [the past] in his own spirit, which is different from the spirit of the object itself" (16).

Barbara, when convincing Hodge to use her time machine, differentiates between these two ways of knowing. She tells Hodge: "You can verify every fact, study every move, every actor. You can write history as no one ever did before, for you'll be writing as a witness, yet with the perspective of a different period. You'll be taking the mind of the present, with its judgment and its knowledge of the patterns, back to receive the impressions of the past" (183).

This remark shows that she understands the relationship between original and reflective history, as well as its tremendous value to historians and the study of the past. When Hodge travels back in time, he hopes to be able to balance original and reflective history. He wants to be there and then fit what he witnesses into the context he learned and draw his own conclusions. By questioning the nature of time and history through time travel, *Jubilee* suggests that the meeting place of time and history, never before conceived of as being literally encounterable by someone outside its arrow, can in fact be bridged and altered. However, Hodge resorts to narrative to make sense of the conflation of time's arrow and time's cycle as a method of coping with his experiences. Hodge, ever the historian, needs narration to make his experiences explicable and coherent.

Jubilee follows the protagonist, the intellectual Hodge Backmaker, from 1931 to 1952. In Moore's bleak world, life after the Peace of Richmond in 1864 has not been kind to the remaining twenty-six states. At the age of seventeen, Hodge moves to New York, where he gets a job in a bookstore, the better to read copiously, as college is out of his reach. He eventually falls in with a crowd of radical intellectuals and joins them in their retreat, Haggershaven, as a historian specializing in the War of Southron Independence. One of the other scholars there, physicist Barbara Haggerwells, granddaughter of the founder of Haggershaven, invents a time machine, the HX-1, and Hodge discovers that he can actually travel to the past and witness the Battle of Gettysburg, the decisive battle that clinched the South's victory. Naturally, he leaps at the chance to witness the battle firsthand.

He leaves in 1952 for July 1863. Though Barbara tells him not to interact with the locals, he inadvertently does so: he refuses to speak to a group of soldiers who spot him at the battle site, and they convince themselves that he is concealing information about the Yanks' position. They retreat, fail to take Round Top, and eventually lose the war. Hodge finds himself trapped in another past, another world. Worse, there is no way to get back, because a soldier shot as a result of his unintentional interference is none other than Barbara's great-great-grandfather. Hodge watches as a new history unfolds—a better history, he believes, but nonetheless one alien to him. The book has a punch line, of course. The new history he has brought into being is *our* history.

By changing his past and thus wiping out his future, Hodge sets the course of events following the Battle of Gettysburg onto another path. This presupposes a linear conception of time, which alternate histories in general do presuppose. Hayden White relies on the notion that the past and the present are separate, but somehow related, things: "the very claim to have distinguished a past from a present world of social thought and praxis . . . *implies* a conception of the form that knowledge of the present world also must take, insofar as it is *continuous* with that past world" (*Metahistory*, 21). Time is a continuum, according to White's conceptualization, that leads from past to present, with events in the past leading to or causing events in the present, which in turn will presumably lead to events in the future. This notion of cause and effect is vital to the conception of time as linear, as time's arrow, and is the metaphor implied in most historical writings.

The concepts of time's arrow and time's cycle—and their attendant metaphors—are pervasive when describing time. Stephen Jay Gould's *Time's Arrow, Time's Cycle* (1987) examines these metaphors in some detail while acknowledging that the metaphors he explores in his study of geologic time are nearly universal. In addition to these notions of time, theologians have also posited the existence of sacred time, which is neither cyclical or linear. David Ewing Duncan defines sacred time as "a kind of antitime that Christians equate with God, who is perfect, eternal, and timeless" and that was associated with the writings of Augustine of Hippo in his *Confessions* and *The City of God* (69). *Bring the Jubilee* does not address this overtly religious time sense, preferring instead to link time's arrow with time's cycle.

White argues that as the historian writes, he or she creates a narrative with "a discernible beginning, middle, and end" (*Metahistory*, 7)—time's arrow. This also implies a point before which the events under discussion do not exist, a point at which they come into being, a point at which the consequences remain in doubt, and a point at which the consequences are clear and irreversible. Alternate histories, particularly those that deal with nexus points, use a like series of cause-and-effect points. In *Jubilee*, time's arrow meets time's cycle. The events take place in a fictive world extrapolated from a past event, then move to a historical world when Moore takes Hodge back in time to explore a nexus event. Here, Moore relies on events already constituted (the Civil War and the Battle of Gettysburg) mixed with invention (Hodge's encounter with Confederate soldiers).

The book concludes with Hodge living safely in our world, trapped in a past that grows more alien as time progresses. We watch as Hodge travels to a past when the consequences did not exist, as the battle had not yet occurred. Next, Hodge meets the soldiers, the point at which the event should come into being but does not; the soldiers retreat. The consequences remain in doubt as Hodge returns to the pickup site, a barn, and remains there in suspense all night, as he is not picked up as planned. Then he realizes that the dead man he saw who looked familiar is Barbara's great-great-grandfather, the founder of Haggershaven, and he knows he has irreversibly wiped out his own world. From this, we can extrapolate our world, just as we extrapolated Hodge's world from its attendant technological differences when faced with the alternate world's bizarre social structure and technology.

Science fiction in particular has solid precedent in dealing with time's arrow, perhaps one thematic reason alternate histories are categorized as science fiction and not something else. Science fiction relies on natural rules and laws that deal with sciences such as physics, biology, astronomy, or linguistics. Writers who posit a story set in the future presuppose time's arrow, suggesting that if events continue as they do, a certain event will result. A good example is Frederik Pohl and C. M. Kornbluth's *The Space Merchants* (1984), a satirical "if this goes on" look at a future world characterized by incessant consumption fueled by go-go advertising. This novel suggests a world of diminishing resources run by ruthless advertising executives—a world, alas, not too hard to imagine. But this reliance on cause and effect is just one way science fiction deals with the linear conception of history. Time's arrow and time's cycle are metaphors that express such a historical law.

Tied to the conception of time's arrow—and one reason it seems unnatural when chronology is disrupted—is the human perception of time, which always views events as occurring linearly. Paul J. Nahin notes of human time sense:

> The special moment at which [the distinction between past and future events] occurs is known as the *now* or the *present*, and as events make the transition associated with this distinctive difference between past and future, the now moves, or flows. Philosophers (and physicists, too) call this common feeling that all humans have of the passage of time the *psychological arrow of time*. (123)

Fictive writings, particularly novels, which attempt to recreate the human condition realistically, including the time-boundedness of the individual, rely on this psychological arrow, the feeling of naturalness that arises from knowing that cause precedes effect. The novelist always creates such constructions out of language and narrative; in this sense, narrative is implicit in human time sense. Narrative is temporally bound.

One important text that attempts to disrupt this "fact" is Martin Amis's *Time's Arrow* (1991), a book that redirects the human time sense. In Amis's novel, a man literally lives life backward: he awakens to consciousness when he dies, then moves backward to the hospital, where he gets steadily better. Then paramedics rush him to his garden, where he blacks out. He then reawakens and gardens for a while. Actions are all backward: People walk backward, drive backward. Even speech is backward. Instead of moving to death of old age, the narrator is moving toward the blackness of loss of consciousness as a child, then loss of life through conception.

However, the narrator's psychological sense of time moves forward. The backward movement seems odd to him, and he expresses time as we do. To him, pimps seem like wonderful people: they remove bruises from prostitutes' faces and give them money. The kicker of the story is the identity of the man. He is a Nazi doctor who worked at the death camp at Auschwitz. However, the doctor's actions are seen here as positive, not negative: the doctor extracts poison from Jews and gypsies. The poisoned showers awaken the dead. The Nazis are responsible for forcibly repatriating the Jews, for dismantling ghettos, and for providing the Jews with greater and greater freedoms. By turning time's arrow around, the horrible becomes the sublime and good becomes evil. However, the direction of the arrow means there is no free will and that the world cannot change, for cause and effect work here too. But with the effect occurring first, the cause is all too inevitable.

Time's arrow relies on a sense of past–present–future and on temporality. Narrative, which has been linked with historiography since modern history began in the 1800s, is the tool used to express linearity and to link it to temporality. F. R. Ankersmit notes of historical narrative, "If the narrative form in which the historian casts his accounts of the past is not subject to change it seems fairly obvious to me that this narrative form must be an important clue to the nature of historical knowing" (11). Narrative is one method used to structure events in order to privilege an inevitable kind of interpretation, an interpretation the teller decides. It is also the method that seems the most natural to our culture. As a result, narrativity tends to strike us as obvious or invisible. To structure events into a story with a beginning, a middle, and an end seems the most natural thing in the world. Indeed, when I teach students the structure of linear narrative, I have a student tell the class about his or her worst experience in a restaurant. Invariably, the student structures the event narratively, with some exposition to set the stage, rising action leading to a climax (the awful event), and a denouement to wrap it up. If the student skips a section, I can use that to my advantage, too, as the student generally goes back to pick up the stray thread.

Lawrence Stone points out that history was considered by the very oldest historians (that is, Thucydides and Tacitus) to be a branch of rhetoric. Stone notes that "narrative is a mode of historical writing, but it is a model which also affects and is affected by the content and the method" (4).

In any case, the role of narrative in historical analysis has been problematized by historians such as Fernand Braudel, associated with the *Annales* school, whose *The Mediterranean and the Mediterranean World in the Age of Philip II* (1949) breaks with the tradition of constructing history as a narrative that Leopold von Ranke advocated when he created "the first 'scientific history' . . . based on the study of new source materials" (Stone, 5). Braudel's important work typifies an "analytical and structural approach" (Stone, 7); one critic describes Braudel's nonnarrative technique as "a deliberate strategy of preferring 'intelligibility' to the 'reality' principle" (Bann, "Analysing," 67). Despite the work of the so-called post–World War II new historians such as Braudel, narrativity has come back into favor, in part because the intellectual framework that sustained the nonnarrative mode shifted. Stone sees the shift back to narrative by historians as "the end of an era: the end of the attempt to produce a coherent scientific explanation of change in the past" (19).

Hayden White's *Metahistory* brought the discussion of narrative back to the fore; most historians see narrative as a nonissue, something so well understood and culturally defined that of course history is told using this rhetorical strategy. Even writers who break with narrative tradition still comment on narration by its conspicuous absence. The point White makes that was controversial is his insistence that historians select the narrative structure to fit their thesis, which calls into question the disinterestedness of the historian.

Nancy F. Partner notes: "Historians are the professional custodians of pattern . . . any series of events (including events of the mind, of large populations, or economic events) which can be described in a single intelligible and significant pattern is a story, and the verbal arrangement that describes the pattern is narrative" ("Making Up," 94).

These historians all see narrative as a culturally accepted patterning device based on language that imposes order on events by structuring events temporally. Literary critics tend to agree with this definition; the difference lies not in the strategy of telling but in the truth claim of the events that are being structured. Time's arrow is the metaphor that underlies narrative structuring.

Susan Wells notes that "narrative permits the complex subjective and objective structuring of time to be laid onto the structures of language" (37). The notion of subject and object is here particularly relevant, because *Jubilee* is written as a first-person memoir, which meshes thematically with this text, because although time loops back on itself and is redirected as Hodge sets a new history into motion, Hodge himself lives linearly within the psychological arrow of time. The world changes around him, but Hodge remains the same, with a normal time sense. He does not, for instance, get younger or die when he goes back in time. For Hodge, time's arrow is still in place. His stilted, logical, historical narrative attempts to make objective sense, in Hodge's best historical mode, of subjective happenings that do not permit normal historical narrative patterning, because the temporal element of time's arrow on which narrative is dependent is not valid in Hodge's experiences. The document he produces is, ironically, a historical trace: history relies on documentation, and Hodge has written the kind of witness account that future historians (such as the reader) will study. Hodge instinctively moves to narrative to make sense of the world around him.

In contrast to this view of time's arrow, time's cycle means that "events have no meaning as distinct episodes with causal impact upon a contingent history. Fundamental states are immanent in time, always present and never changing. . . . Time has no direction" (Gould, 11). In narrative writings, this conception of time generally occurs when the writer disrupts cause and effect, sometimes through devices such as stream of consciousness. Gould concludes his discussion of these two metaphors by noting that both are necessary, since they describe different but complementary ways of viewing time: "time's arrow is the intelligibility of distinct and irreversible events, while time's cycle is the intelligibility of timeless order and lawlike structure. We must have both" (15–16).

Jubilee draws on both these metaphors thematically, implying "timeless order" as well as "distinct and irreversible events." The narrative structure parallels these thematic concerns. Hodge uses his subjective time sense to structure his memoirs, so the story is told in "chronological" order only in that Hodge writes of events in the order he experienced them. However, because Moore uses time travel, the novel is not literally chronological: Hodge leaps from 1952 to 1863. By doing this, *Jubilee* seeks to deflect the path of time's arrow, causing it to turn back on itself and then take a new course. Cause and effect are still in place, but because of Hodge's presence in the peach orchard at the site of the Battle of Gettysburg, the arrow is redirected and brings about a different outcome, the North winning the Civil War. The fact that history changes means that "timeless order and lawlike structure" are called into question; changing the very course of history means that history is mutable, which calls into question the concepts of order and structure.

As discussed previously, narrative is so much a part of our culture that it is hard to conceive of structuring time without it, since this is the role of narrative. The narrative structure of this novel parallels the theories of history that Moore explores through Hodge, whose subjectivity is of interest here. The novel begins and ends in the same time and place, since the story is told retrospectively. The novel opens: "Although I am writing this in the year 1877, I was not born until 1921. Neither the dates nor the tenses are [in] error—let me explain" (11). This framing device concludes with the last chapter: "I am writing this, as I said, in 1877. I am a healthy man of forty-five, no doubt with many years ahead of me. I might live to be a hundred, except for an illogical feeling that I must die before 1921," the year of his birth (218). The narrative is linear, bound by Hodge's pattern of experience and his own psychological time sense, but the framing device implies circularity: Hodge begins and ends in the same place. Time's arrow and time's cycle coexist here, and the novel refuses to resolve.

Hodge's memoirs break off a line or two after this passage. Hodge, and the novel, fail to conclude satisfactorily. The narrative ends suddenly, literally in midsentence, as suddenly as Hodge's world disappeared in an ill-timed encounter. The book concludes with a section written in 1953 by Frederick Winter Thammis, a descendent of the man Hodge worked for in his exile, noting that Hodge frequently told long, rambling stories about "an impossible world" (221). However, he provides proof and corroboration of Hodge's history: a historical artifact with symbolic value. Thammis writes, "In the box of Backmaker's belongings there was a watch of unknown manufacture and unique design. Housed in a cheap nickel case, the jeweled movement is of extraordinary precision and delicacy. The face has two dials, independently set and wound" (221). Readers recognize it as the watch Barbara gave Hodge before he stepped into the HX-1, with the dials representing the times of Hodge's present and his past. This is all that remains of the lost history—now a lost future.

Jubilee questions the solidity of time's arrow. For Hodge, time is still linear; Hodge has just started the arrow on a new path. *Jubilee*'s history-gone-awry theme foregrounds the precariousness of established history by allowing Hodge to change it easily in a chance encounter in a peach orchard, something many alternate histories sidestep by envisioning historical events as difficult or impossible to change. Mark Rose points out that "the alternate history novel generally regards history as a more or less arbitrary causal sequence. *Bring the Jubilee* suggests that if matters had fallen out only slightly otherwise at Gettysburg, the entire world would be different. . . . Moreover, behind the alternate history is still another version of the Pascalian vertigo, the dizzying vision of the infinite possibilities of times that might have been" (119). *Jubilee* reverses this. The time that might have been, for Hodge, is our world. Redirecting the arrow of time implies that whereas time is still linear, it may not be a solid, unbroken line.

The vision of *Jubilee* is not quite as dizzying, as Moore implies that only at nexus events can events be changed. In the book, some Haggershaven scholars had already traveled back in the past and had returned safely, without altering the past. Hodge himself fails to change the world in other ways; in fact, he has a hard time imagining how he could technologically affect the new world, because technology seems to be moving in different directions following the war than it had in his world. He expresses skepticism that electricity could work better than gaslight and wonders about the future existence of minibles and balloons. He does not attempt to reproduce the inventions of his world; not only does he lack the technical skill, but he also notes that he does not want the money (220).

By writing a "history" of a time that never was, Moore indicates the importance of cause and effect. If the South wins the War of Southron Independence, then Emperor Napoleon VI rules France; the Emperor's War occurred in 1914–16; and the United States exists in abject poverty, with indentured servitude and slavery, gaslit homes, and communication via telegraph. The cascade of events following the war results just sixty-seven years later in an incomprehensible landscape, which Moore renders in some detail through his pedantic protagonist. But by writing a fantastic history, Moore critiques the linear conception of history, stating that the arrow can be turned and that in fact, it is quite easy to do so. There is a reason Hodge is a historian: he uses a historian's eye to detail and a historian's methods to examine his own world, realizing that "not chronology but relationship is ultimately what the historian deals in" (138)—an interesting comment, as it articulates the goal of some of the *Annales* historians. For Hodge, time blurs as he delves into his object of study in the past and makes it present; then he makes this literal as the HX-1 takes him into the past.

Moore queries these assumptions by using time's arrow and time's cycle as themes. Hodge's discussions with his bookseller boss, Tyss, revolve around Tyss's perception of time as an endlessly repeating loop, with history and time as cyclic. To Tyss, humans respond only to stimuli, with "every action . . . the rigid result of another action"; he asks, "What makes you think time is a simple straight line running flatly through eternity? Why do you assume that time isnt curved? Can you conceive of its end? Can you really imagine its beginning? Of course not; then why arent both the same? The serpent with its tail in its mouth?" Hodge responds to this by saying, "You mean we not only play a prepared script but repeat the identical lines over and over and over for infinity?" (51). However, Tyss is right. The time travel machine, the HX-1, proves that time can curve, if made to do so.

Hodge's discussions with Haitian diplomat René Enfandin, on the other hand, call Tyss's beliefs into question; Enfandin prefers to give power to God. Enfandin remarks of Tyss: "He has liberated himself from the superstitions of religion in order to fall into superstition so abject no Christian can conceive it. . . . The answer is that all—time, space, matter—all is illusion. All but the good God Himself. Nothing is real but Him. We are creatures of His fancy, figments of His imagination." When Hodge questions him about the role of free will in such a universe, Enfandin responds that free will is a "gift," or possibly supernatural, arguing that it is "the greatest gift and the greatest responsibility" (75). Enfandin's notion of reality as a figment of God's imagination allows for free will that is given as a gift from God, thus making possible individual determination, something Hodge finds appealing—certainly more appealing than Tyss's staunch belief that individuals must experience the same events over and over again, reacting reliably to stimuli, devoid of free will.

Important to these ideas of free will and action is Hodge himself. Consistently unable to make decisions, he prefers to wait until an outside force makes decisions for him. Tyss calls him "the spectator type" (195). When a university scholarship that Enfandin arranges for Hodge falls through at the last minute, Hodge does not tell Tyss, though Hodge had given notice; instead, he remains at the bookstore until Barbara Haggerwells comes to interview him and invites him to Haggershaven. His greatest capitulation of responsibility is when he refuses to tell his wife, Catty, that he is going back in time to do research, rationalizing that he will be back soon and she will never know. Instead, he tells her that he plans to visit a battle site and will be gone a few days. He imagines he hears Tyss's voice telling him, *"Free will is an illusion; you cannot alter what you are about to decide under the impression that you have decided"* (195). Furious at Tyss and at himself, he decides to go, noting: "The decision had been made. Not by mechanistic forces, nor by blind response to stimulus, but by my own desire" (195). Later, as the Confederate soldiers confront him, Hodge realizes that not acting, not speaking, is a kind of choice; his very passivity could be said to be a way of making a choice. When his choice has repercussions, he realizes that even a single individual's actions can dramatically alter the world.

When Hodge changes the course of a battle and thus changes the outcome of the war, he immediately thinks of Tyss. Is Hodge doomed to spend eternity repeatedly wiping out his own world at the expense of another? Hodge wonders: "What of Tyss's philosophy? Is it possible I shall be condemned to repeat the destruction throughout eternity? Have I written these lines an infinite number of times before? Or is the mercy envisaged by Enfandin a reality?" (220–21). Moore never answers this central question. Hodge asks himself:

> Are they really gone, irrevocably lost, in a future which never existed, which couldnt exist, once the chain of causation was broken? Or do they exist after all, in a universe in which the South won the battle of Gettysburg and Major Haggerwells founded Haggershaven? . . . Once lost, that particular past can never be regained. Another and another perhaps, but never the same one. There are no parallel universes — though this one may be sinuous and inconstant. (219)

Moore here dismisses the notion of multiple parallel histories coexisting temporally, diverging from each other in their nexus events. After Hodge's trip in time, history resumes its linear course. The only place the other history exists is in Hodge's memory and in Hodge's historical narrative. Indeed, Hodge's first-person narrative is structured in such a way that the twist at the end (the new history is our history) calls into question the truth claim of the events, further blurring the distinction between history and fiction.

The HX-1 implies that time is "sinuous and inconstant." Barbara's time machine allows linear time to loop back upon itself and figuratively redirect the arrow. Alternate histories in general rely on a history based on cause and effect in a changeable universe. Only with hindsight—by retrospection and thought—can Hodge see the critical nature of certain events, events he structures as a narrative. In his world, the South taking Round Top clinched the Southron victory, but Hodge needs retrospection and the distance of time in order to fit the battle into a context. He loses retrospection when he changes history and becomes a participant instead of an observer. He ceases to act as a historian writing reflective history and instead becomes a purveyor of original history, as his memoirs imply.

Thanks to Hodge's ill-timed encounter, history has become our own, the tension between what we know to be true and what Moore writes of has been resolved, but Hodge's questions regarding the nature of time and history are never answered. Is Hodge destined to repeat the same actions over and over, or has he broken through the loop of causation by destroying his universe altogether? Hodge's great hope is that "there must have been a beginning. . . . And if there was a beginning, choice existed if only for that split second. And if choice exists once it can exist again" (51). Indeed, the circularity of the structure of the novel begs the question of a beginning. Nancy F. Partner could be speaking of Hodge's attempt to make meaning when she writes: "Our first and last consolation, our primal defiance of the endless pointlessness of successive time, is the secret insistence on seeing our own life as a story, our own birth and death imposing a beginning and an end on the formless flow of time, charging the middle with meaning, with plot and tension. . . . determined to read the story into conscious significance before consciousness fails" ("Making Up," 91). Hodge's writing is an attempt to construct an arrow when Hodge fears that time's cycle is the true metaphor underlying the phenomenon of time.

However, cannot Tyss's notion and Hodge's wish for true freedom both be true? Mark Rose notes that "the paradox at the heart of the time loop is that both free will and determinism are asserted simultaneously, for here genuinely free agents are nevertheless caught in cycles of determined repetition" (109). Though Rose speaks here of causal time loops, where an event set in motion brings about the event itself, his remark might also apply to *Jubilee* and its play with time's cycle. Hodge asserts free will—or thinks he does—but he concludes that he cannot know if he is part of an endless repetition or if he is truly capable of making decisions that ripple through history, irrevocably changing it. Hodge never gets his answer.

Though *Jubilee* never lets the reader know if Hodge is genuinely free or caught in a cycle of repetition, Hodge's understanding that he is capable of making decisions implies that personal understanding can transcend the true nature of history, whatever that might be. History, dependent on time, may be an arrow or a cycle—perhaps both—but Hodge needs to come to terms with his place in the universe. When he does so, the time question becomes irrelevant, for Hodge has finally changed. Moore thus implies that perhaps history itself is irrelevant; perhaps the real relevance is the historian and what he makes of these events. The constructing, not the final construct, is the point.

3 | Parallel Worlds: Simultaneity and Time

> There is more than one future we can encounter, and with more or less
> absence of deliberation we choose among them. But the futures we
> fail to encounter, upon the roads we do not take, are just as real as the
> landmarks upon the roads.
> —Murray Leinster, "Sidewise in Time"

Chapter 2 concluded that for Ward Moore, the construction of history, not
history itself, is the point of history making. The protagonist of *Bring the
Jubilee* (1955), the historian Hodge, discovers this when he becomes the
agent of his world's destruction—and of another world's creation. Hodge
alters a cause and brings about another effect—a new world—thereby redirecting the arrow of time. For this reason, Moore's novel is concerned with
the genetic theory of history, as it deals with causes. When Moore destroys
Hodge's alternate world and brings about our own, however, he deliberately cuts off any hope that Hodge's world exists somewhere.

The parallel worlds story, however, allows this to occur. The parallel
worlds story also relies on the genetic theory of history, as it posits a universe populated by an uncountable number of worlds that exist simultaneously with our own, each the product of a different effect springing
from any given cause. David K. Danow argues that linear texts can be
interrupted "from present to past," "from present to the distant . . . future,"

and "from either past or future back to the present" (28). The parallel worlds story seeks to avoid this kind of structure, instead moving from the present to the present, resulting in a different kind of chronology. The notion of parallel worlds can be linked to the counterfactual idea of modal realism, "which holds that numerous possible worlds of histories *exist*, in which some of them do not fulfill any particular teleological scheme of history" (Tucker, 267). Parallel worlds therefore have the capability to cast notions of history seriously into doubt, as the meaning of history in another world can be troublingly other.

Because of the nature of the breaks that result in another time line, parallel worlds alternate histories rely on agency, or the bringing about of action by someone, as agents cause actions to happen. Turning right on the street instead of left, a trivial action, could result in two dramatically different effects and two dramatically different worlds years later. Poul Anderson writes in his Time Patrol novel *The Shield of Time* (1990): "Beneath reality lies ultimate quantum indeterminacy. On the level of observable happenings it manifests itself as chaos in the physics sense of the word, the fact that often immeasurably small forces bring illimitably large consequences" (163). Anderson is talking about the structure of time, but parallel worlds stories use this same idea for the structure of parallel realities. The metaphor writers use most often to explain parallel worlds is quantum physics.

Physicist John Wheeler popularized the use of quantum physics to explain simultaneous alternate worlds. So many science fiction writers have picked up on it that linking quantum physics and parallel worlds has become a cliché. In *The Coming of the Quantum Cats* (1986), Frederik Pohl, famous as a writer for his clear and easy-to-grasp explanations of complex scientific ideas, summarizes the theory used to describe the possibility of parallel worlds:

> Suppose you put a cat in a box, said Schroedinger. Suppose you put in with the cat a radioactive particle, which has exactly one chance in two of fissioning. Suppose in with the cat and the radionuclide, you put a can of poison gas with a switch that will be triggered if the particle fissions. Then you look at the outside of the box and ask yourself if the cat is alive or dead. If the particle has fissioned, it's dead. If the particle hasn't fissioned, the gas was not released and the cat is alive.
>
> But from outside there is no knowing which is true. . . . So . . . the point is that both things are true. The cat's alive. The cat's dead. But

each statement is true in a particular universe. At the point of decision the universes split—and now, forever after, there will be parallel universes. A cat-alive universe, and a cat-dead universe. (69)

An infinite number of universes is thereby created, depending on the fissioning of the particle—or, to extend this idea, as science fiction writers do, depending on the outcome of any event, no matter how trivial. In addition to the cat-alive, cat-dead universe multiplicity it implies, this theory, called the collapse of the wave function, also holds that the act of observing will force a change to be made. The moment of decision that Pohl mentions is the moment when the observer opens the box to look at the cat (Nicholls, "Alternative Universes," 100). At that moment, the cat will be either alive or dead. The act of observing forces a split (Baringer, personal communication).

Michael Crichton, in *Timeline* (1999), uses quantum mechanics to explain why travel through time is possible. He posits the reality of a multiverse accessible to researchers who make "wormhole connections" in "subatomic fluctuations of space-time," or quantum foam (109). In short, in this novel, researchers have found a way to move from one universe to another in a way that is not time travel but that has the same results. Crichton limits the field of multiverse travel by limiting it to other universes very similar to the one in question and by disallowing any kind of time paradox. Interestingly, Crichton views this technology as a way to significantly move forward the field of the humanities, seeing it as a new technology that can assist literary scholars and historians—although of course there is also the ability of this technology to make money.

Contrast with this either-or metaphor from physics one that ups the ante: chaos theory. Chaos theory relies on extremely complex systems. The classic metaphor for chaos theory is that of a butterfly's wings resulting in dramatic effects on the weather: a small flap disturbs the air and later has a profound effect on a hurricane. Chaos theory is a good way to explain the parallel worlds story because both rely on the reality of small changes. In chaos theory, small changes are magnified tremendously over time, resulting in a changed complex system, such as weather. In parallel worlds, each small change can literally be true, resulting in a multiplicity of worlds, all different, that have sprung from different causes. The link between chaos theory and history has not gone unremarked; Johannes Bulhof argues that history, like the weather, is a complex system: "It is irreversible, and so is most likely chaotic. Small disturbances in certain contexts can have profound effects that are unpredictable" (162). The parallel worlds story plays with these unpredictable historical events, magnifying small changes by analyzing complex structures (such as societies) that have occurred years after a changed event.

Although the notion of parallel worlds that I outline above seems to indicate that parallel worlds are the result of changes in a complex system or the result of observing (or not observing) a quantum event, not all parallel worlds take this tack. Some foreground the agency of humans: the individual may bring about the move from one alternate reality to another. The most important example is Roger Zelazny's ambitious Amber series, which begins with *Nine Princes in Amber* (1970). In these texts, certain characters have the capability to move from one parallel world to another by shaping thoughts. Using a related theme, Élisabeth Vonarburg's *Reluctant Voyagers* (1994) tells of a planet, seemingly an alternate world, controlled by some of the people who inhabit it. The people who inhabit it are themselves from a parallel universe, and they have the power to shape the planet into whatever they like, thus creating a world in their image.

Instead of strictly historical events, alternate histories and parallel worlds may also play with what we consider fundamental truths: the existence of fixed physical laws or rules that govern such sciences as cosmology and physics. For instance, parallel worlds may exist in which Planck's constant differs from ours, or gravity behaves differently, because of some small change when the world was created. One rich example (although not a parallel worlds story) is Richard Garfinkle's *Celestial Matters* (1996), which posits a world based on different physical laws than ours. Likewise, in Philip José Farmer's "Sail On! Sail On!" (1952), Columbus's theory that the earth is round is proved wrong when his fleet sails off the edge of the world. Neil F. Comins has written alternate histories that posit an altered solar system (for instance, if the Earth had less mass); these stories have been collected in *What If the Moon Didn't Exist? Voyages to Earths that Might Have Been* (1993). Max P. Belin calls these kinds of alternate histories "pocket universes" because they have different physical laws convenient for the telling of the story (236). Or the parallel worlds may splinter off as a result of bizarre events that imply outside agency, such as aliens landing and taking over Earth before Earth-based sentient life evolves (as in H. Beam Piper's Paratime works). Other parallel worlds texts include Murray Leinster's "Sidewise in Time" (1934), the short story that introduced the parallel worlds story to science fiction; Sam Merwin Jr.'s *The House of Many Worlds* (1951) and *Three Faces of Time* (1955); Andre

Norton's *The Crossroads of Time* (1956); Keith Laumer's *Worlds of the Imperium* (1962); Richard C. Meredith's Timeliner trilogy, which begins with *At the Narrow Passage* (1979); Phyllis Eisenstein's *Shadow of Earth* (1979); Andrew M. Stephenson's *The Wall of Years* (1979); L. Neil Smith's *The Probability Broach* (1980) and *The Crystal Empire* (1986); Sheila Finch's *Infinity's Web* (1985); and George Alec Effinger's Hugo and Nebula award–winning "Schrödinger's Kitten" (1988).

Though the time-as-arrow metaphor is important to the notion of parallel worlds, parallel worlds stories change the focus from a one-way direction of time—the past moving to the future—to a sideways (or crosswise) direction of time, into another "stream" that also moves from past to future. It is true, however, that many of the time lines that are literally simultaneous are metaphorically "future" or "past," depending on the level of technology present in parallel worlds. For instance, Sam Merwin Jr. writes in *Three Faces of Time* (1955) of a world called Antique that lies parallel to the protagonist's world but that, through bizarre cosmic disaster, has lost about two thousand years, so that many famed people and events of a distant era exist alongside people who consider them to be historical figures. Phyllis Eisenstein's bleak *Shadow of Earth* (1979) has a traveler move to a parallel America, colonized by the Spanish, that seems to be stuck in the Middle Ages.

Parallel worlds novels do not subvert the question of time; rather, they add another dimension to discussions about the nature of time. Most significantly, they posit a multiplicity of worlds that may be virtually identical, right down to the people who inhabit them. Only slight differences may differentiate two worlds. This chapter will examine simultaneous time as expressed in H. Beam Piper's Paratime works, with reference to Frederik Pohl's *The Coming of the Quantum Cats* (1986). I will discuss parallel worlds in terms of the individual's intervening in historical events—that is, I will discuss individual agency, or the ability of a person to act or bring about the occurrence of events through action, and I will relate this notion of agency to a narrative structure that relies on simultaneity.

Parallel worlds are the best kind of text to use when discussing individual agency because they allow all events to happen simultaneously. Many parallel worlds works allow several versions of the same person to exist, even to meet. These duplicate people are called analogues. Frederik Pohl calls them "cats" in *The Coming of the Quantum Cats* (thus the title), a reference to Schrödinger's cat-alive and cat-dead universes. Keith Laumer plays with the idea of analogues in *Worlds of the Imperium* (1962), where an analogue is kidnapped in one world to replace an important person in another. Thus, depending on how events occurred, an analogue may be an ordinary citizen in one world but an important ruler in another. All possibilities literally exist, and these occur on the personal level as well as the broader historical level.

The infinite number of analogues that exist in parallel worlds stories calls into question notions of agency and free will. Stories such as Robert Heinlein's famous "All You Zombies—" (1959) descend into solipsism: all the characters in "Zombies" are the protagonist, who travels in time and changes sex, becoming his own mother and father. "Zombies" uses a circular structure: the protagonist has no free will and is destined to repeat the same events over and over. Paul A. Carter notes that parallel worlds do not resolve the question of free will, because both still exist; the person exerting the free will exists in both, and the past still exists in each world, unchangeable (110). In contrast, Bud Foote finds only two kinds of meaning in parallel worlds stories. Since parallel worlds allow every possibility to coexist, he argues, "either all existence and all choice are mere illusion" or "in some sense all possible time lines are truly real, and therefore no choice can have any possible meaning" (10). In either case, nothing can have meaning. Foote finds parallel worlds to subvert morality, since he argues that a horrible deed punished in one time line may, in a parallel line, go unpunished. Why not commit crimes when, in another world, they never happened?

I find Foote's argument faulty because he fails to take into account the subjectivity of the separate analogues. Like clones, they are the same genetic material acted upon differently by environment. One analogue does not share his or her analogues' consciousness. I agree with David Wood, who, speaking of time and multidimensionality, notes: "In the world of texts and discursive sequences, there is no *one* time. Multidimensionality is the rule. . . . And yet multidimensionality does not require the sacrifice of the intentional—of meaning, horizons and so forth—rather its expansion" (339). Parallel worlds stories take multidimensionality and expansion of horizons literally.

H. Beam Piper's Paratime sequence of stories is collected in *Lord Kalvan of Otherwhen* (1965) and *Paratime* (1981), both of which are made up of short stories or novelettes originally published in science fiction magazines from the late 1940s until 1965 (Piper killed himself in 1964). John F. Carr and Roland J. Green wrote several sequels to Piper's Lord Kalvan stories, including *Great Kings' War* (1985) and "Kalvan Kingmaker" (1989). I do not discuss these two texts. Paratime is simply Piper's term for parallel worlds. *Lord Kalvan* tells stories about Calvin Morrison, a police officer presumably from our world who accidentally gets caught in a Paratimer machine that dumps him into a parallel world, where his superior knowledge and abilities allow him to quickly become an important ruler. The Lord Kalvan stories are about an unsavory theocracy, Styphon's House, that controls the manufacture of gunpowder and thus rules a low-technology world; Piper tells how Kalvan beats the theocracy. The stories in *Lord Kalvan* and *Paratime* all take place in the same reality: one time line has discovered the secret of moving from one parallel world to the next, and these Paratimers exploit all the other time lines to support themselves.

Piper divides his parallel worlds into levels, based on their proximity and likeness to the home time line—"home" being the home of the only race in Paratime that has discovered the secret of moving to parallel worlds. Piper's time divisions are useful because they cover both large- and small-scale spectra of probability. Piper's parallel worlds organization takes into account methodological individualism and holism, two historical theories. The former allows individuals to drive history. The latter takes a larger view, with individuals only existing to form groups. These groups then bring about events that we might call history (Munz, 226–27). Holism, with its focus on groups or societies, is the idea behind the five areas of probability that Piper uses to organize time most grossly.

The five areas spring from their closeness to or distance from the Martian colonization of Earth after the inhabitants of Mars used up the resources on their world seventy-five thousand years ago. The First Level is that of total success, with the Martians safely on Earth and their integration complete. The Fifth Level is that of total failure, with indigenous quasi-human life evolving. (We are in the Fourth Level—we have advanced technology but are under the illusion that we are indigenous to Earth.) Within the levels are sectors, or structures of society that have common features. These are divided arbitrarily into subsectors and finally belts. Belts are differentiated from one another by individual-level minutiae: the outcome of a fight, the presence or absence of a knife at a scene. In "Time Crime," the Paratime Police investigate a cross-belt Paratime slave trade, fixing the home time line of the slaves by close hypnotic questioning of the captured slaves, ferreting out which slaves came from a world where a woman killed herself and which came from a world where she was captured alive.

The stories in *Paratime* do not focus on any one alternate world but explore a number of them; my favorite is "Last Enemy," which takes place in the Akor-Neb civilization, a Second Level civilization in which reincarnation is a fact. A Paratime researcher, Dalla, is caught up in a battle between two rival political factions: the Volitionalists, who believe people can choose the next body to inhabit and who therefore support a government that favors inherited wealth, and the Statisticalists, who believe people cannot choose their next body and who thus support a socialist system. John Carr, in his introduction to *Paratime*, notes that Piper was drawn to the time theories of J. W. Dunne, who studied his own dreams and from them posited the existence of "supertime," which, Carr notes, "measures the rate at which time passes" (5). A large number of supertimes exist simultaneously; Dunne created a "supermind" to negotiate them. Dunne's popular-philosophy books, *An Experiment with Time* (1927) and *The New Immortality* (1938), "purported to demonstrate, through mathematics, the immortality of the soul and the principle of serialism (that the individual passes through a single sequence of time as he lives, but that all other times and places exist simultaneously always)" ("Dunne," 282). Although few parallel worlds stories articulate this philosophy in exactly these terms, they do acknowledge the internal time consciousness of the individual while allowing all times and places to exist at once. The parallel worlds theory takes Dunne's notion a step further by allowing all *possible* times and places to exist simultaneously.

Piper's Paratime works, like Poul Anderson's Time Patrol works discussed in chapter 7, create worlds policed by a force charged with protecting its own identity and keeping that identity secret. The culture that created the Paratime Police exploits the alternate time lines it can reach, treating these other worlds as endless sources of raw materials and other resources while upholding strict codes that do not allow anyone to reveal the secret to others. The Paratimers do not allow unauthorized people to be transported from one time line to another, although this happens accidentally sometimes, as the protagonist of *Lord Kalvan* discovers. Similarly, Anderson's Time Patrol protects the time lanes and allows its odd and mysterious founders, the Danellians, to come into being. The Paratimers, on the other hand, cannot move into the present or past but instead must move sideways, into worlds where alternate historical events occur. Piper discusses the simultaneity of the people inhabiting the worlds only briefly; in "Police Operation," a guard examines Verkan Vall's blood under a microscope to make sure he is the right Verkan Vall. The Paratimers inject infants with a substance that stays in their blood during their lifetime. Verkan Vall is thus set apart "from all the myriad other Verkan Valls on every other probability-line of paratime" (48).

The focus on individuals in the Paratime sequence is implicit, although most of the stories read as adventure stories in well-drawn exotic locales. Because the major characters belong to the Paratime Police, they are responsible for taking action in order to solve problems. The story that best explores notions of agency is "Last Enemy," mentioned above, in which reincarnation is an established fact that governs an entire civilization. This short story directly discusses the notion of the individual and his or her ability to take action. The story focuses on the brilliant Dalla, a Paratime researcher who travels in disguise to a Second Level civilization. This civilization has built its entire culture around reincarnation. Piper draws a fascinating picture of various feuding political parties arguing over the autonomy of discarnate entities. Dalla proves absolutely, in front of witnesses, that discarnate entities have free will and can choose to reincarnate advantageously. This throws the entire Akor-Neb civilization into disarray, and Dalla finds herself pursued by the Society of Assassins. Verkan Vall, a Paratime Police operative and Dalla's lover, rushes in and saves her, but not until after Piper has his characters muse about the nature of reincarnation. One character points out the problem with an individual's actually reincarnating advantageously: "Unable to endure the fifty or so years needed to make a really good reincarnation, he reincarnates in a year or so, out of pure boredom, into the first vehicle he can find, usually one nobody else wants" (103). Dalla's findings, backed with a technique for bringing the memories of past lives to the fore, swing the balance of power to one political side. However, Dalla and Verkan Vall find comfort in the chaos into which Dalla has thrown the Akor-Neb civilization: memory retrieval will dissolve time-boundedness, as information learned in a previous lifetime can be retrieved, allowing the individual to pick up where he or she left off. Dalla tells Verkan Vall, "By proving that death is just a cyclic condition of continued individual existence, these people have conquered their last enemy" (146).

The members of this civilization conquer death in two ways. First, they are capable of maintaining memories between reincarnations; though Dalla's research results in a technique that will permit memory retrieval, this kind of retrieval is not yet widespread. Second, they maintain memories while discarnate; they float like ghosts around maternity hospitals (which are popular dueling sites), waiting for a baby to be born so they can reincarnate themselves. Discarnate entities can communicate with the living through particular kinds of media. The individual controls his or her destiny, able to bring about a desired result with a bit of patience and luck. A discarnation by assassination or accident will only result in a temporary setback. Though the civilization is in transition as a result of Dalla's very public research, the characters are all capable of control of themselves and of actions even when discarnate.

The individuals of the Akor-Neb civilization thus express agency on the personal level, as they freely choose their next existence. Paratimers express agency on a larger level. Paratimers are the only civilization that has found the secret of Paratime. They move easily from parallel world to parallel world, manipulating lesser civilizations for their own personal gain. They freely admit that they are parasites living off the resources of an infinite number of other worlds. To keep those resources flowing, they have built up extensive supply lines by posing as natives, taking control of religions and trade guilds, and in general appropriating enough power for themselves to unobtrusively spirit out wealth and raw materials.

The covert power that Paratimers wield contrasts with the power Pennsylvania police officer Calvin Morrison finds himself exercising when he accidentally gets caught in a Paratimer's Ghaldron-Hesthor Transportation Field and is dropped off in a nearby parallel world. As the title of the work implies, *Lord Kalvan of Otherwhen* tells the story of Calvin's exploits as he gathers power, transforms himself into Kalvan, and ends up ruling his new world. The Paratimers watch as Kalvan uses his superior knowledge of practical science, history, and battle to become a leader. In fact, several historians from the home time line study Kalvan because he proves what a Paratime historian calls the "Historical Inevitability" theory of history: "the decisive effect of one superior individual on the course of history" (147), what we might also call the Great Man theory of history. Although Kalvan has penetrated the Paratime secret—that of lateral time shifting, for Kalvan quickly figures out that he has not traveled in time— the Paratimers find him too valuable a study aid to destroy.

Lord Kalvan has as its thesis the notion of human agency. Kalvan is able to literally drop down on an alien world and make something for himself out of it. The world he shifts to, while of course an alternate Earth, is not as advanced technologically as his own world; in fact, making gunpowder is a well-kept secret, with the theocracy that sells it controlling the supply and thus keeping the leaders of the world on a short leash. Luckily, Kalvan had an interest in warfare in college and learned much of practical value, including how to make gunpowder. Kalvan becomes a nobleman who marries a beautiful princess, his rewards for his intelligence and bravery. His transfer to a parallel world was the best thing that ever happened to him, for it allowed free range of his interests and skills in a world that could use those talents.

From the first moment he falls into an alternate Pennsylvania, Kalvan acts. He does not understand what happened to him, but he lands on his feet and gains allies quickly by joining a battle the night he arrives. He quickly becomes a valued battle tactician and inventor. Paul Ricoeur, speaking of human action, asks, "How do we start a movement? By producing the initial state, by exercising a power or capacity, by *intervening* in the course of things" (Ricoeur, "Explanation," 159). Likewise, narrative requires the intervention of agency. Writing fiction or writing history means that narrative will be structured around the notion of intervention. In history, it is the story told about an action taken in the past and expressed by its trace, the document. Ricoeur says of "unique history," "To follow a history is a completely specific activity by which we continuously anticipate a final course and an outcome, and we successively correct our expectations until they coincide with the actual outcome. Then we say that we have understood" (Ricoeur, "Explanation," 164).

As regards agency in the alternate history, the narrative plays with rules of both history and fiction. *Lord Kalvan* is of course clearly fiction, but, as in all alternate histories, history plays an important role. When speaking of unique history, Ricoeur does not expect the reader to be unsurprised during the retelling of historical events, but the narrative must be put together in such a way that the reader can figure out cause and effect— how events that occurred in the past can be interpreted and reinterpreted to bring about the thesis the historian has in mind. Ricoeur is not necessarily speaking of the reader's familiarity with the outcome of a historical moment and fitting the cause-and-effect pattern of the narrative that the historian weaves into an already existing paradigm.

In *Lord Kalvan*, the sense of alienness, the sense of cause and effect that we as readers try to figure out in order to contextualize the novel, is represented by the world Kalvan is thrust into. We are from the same world as Kalvan, and like Kalvan, we attempt to figure out what kind of place this new world is. Kalvan quickly learns he has not traveled to the past when he realizes his new friends worship three unfamiliar gods and speak a language much different from any he knows of. But the giveaway is another symbol of human agency: Kalvan can find no sign of the earthworks and quarries that characterize the Pennsylvania area he is from, leading him to the conclusion that he has moved sideways in time, not backward.

The narrative of the alternate history story takes as its most fundamental base the notion that human agency is important enough to result in dramatically different histories. This results in a sense of personal importance, as even the slightest action has world-shattering consequences. Parallel worlds novels such as *Lord Kalvan* are the kind of fantasy stories that are one expression of this belief that we are important and can make a difference in the world and in the unfolding of events that make up what someone later will call history.

Though Piper divides the uncountable number of parallel worlds into a mere five large intellectual sections, which seems to imply that all of individual human striving results in only one of five outcomes, *Lord Kalvan* argues that individual agency is crucial to the making of history. The narrative of the alternate history seeks to make plausible the individual's role in history making by exaggerating the events that we each individually bring about; the narrative of *Lord Kalvan* strings together a number of cause-and-effect elements, some quite implausible, that result in the dramatic sociopolitical overhaul of a world by a single man. The Paratimers find this kind of individual agency important too: they use the time line that Kalvan has affected to study the role of human agency in history making.

Like Piper's Paratime stories, Frederik Pohl's *The Coming of the Quantum Cats* tells the story of encroachments from one parallel world to another as several Earths discover the technology that permits them to move among parallel worlds. A number of analogues of the same few characters get caught up in parallel world traveling, some for scientific research, some accidentally, some to conquer. Just when the characters realize that the "skin" between the worlds grows thinner with each lateral move, which may result in uncontrolled merging of parallel worlds, they are kidnapped by members of a technologically and morally superior parallel world who have been watching them. They are placed in an empty world in a deserted city. People from this superior time line stop all parallel world hopping and kidnap scientists from a number of different worlds in order to shut down research. All the characters must begin life anew.

Whereas Piper implies that parallel worlds lie flat, with the Paratime Police cutting perpendicularly across the worlds to travel from one to the other, Pohl sees the parallel worlds as a kind of spring with beads on it. The beads may be numbered sequentially, with numbers next to each other implying alikeness, but the spring structure may mean that two beads that would be otherwise unrelated may touch instead. So unlike Piper, who sees nearness as implying alikeness, Pohl puts very different worlds near each other. He mitigates this difference, however, by limiting the range of the device that allows travel from parallel world to parallel world: only worlds with a nexus point about ninety years in the past permit travel, though some other worlds can be looked at. This means that the worlds Pohl discusses are understandable. For instance, in one parallel world,

President Reagan is Nancy Reagan, not Ronald. Indeed, in a disclaimer preceding the novel, Pohl writes, "the characters portrayed are what the real-life characters would have been . . . if they had been someone other than the persons they were" (v).

Unlike Piper, who mentions the notion of analogues only once in his Paratime Police stories, Pohl makes much use of them. One Dominic De-Sota is a member of Congress. One sells mortgages in a moralistic, puritanic world. Several are physicists. All are the same person, acted upon differently by their different environments. Pohl uses a first-person narrative structure that moves from cat to cat to explain the events from his or her own point of view. There is no "original" Dominic (or Dom or Nick), though I suspect that as readers, we would be likely to choose as a protagonist either the first Dominic we meet or the one from the world the closest to our world. But picking sides defeats the purpose of Pohl's narrative structure. Each of the Dominics is his own person, and each deals with his world differently. There is no "original" Dominic—or, rather, every one is an original.

Though the narrative structure of *Quantum Cats* is chronological and linear, Pohl shifts the point of view from character to character. This technique permits simultaneity, as Pohl thus tells stories of a number of different worlds and characters in tandem. Though the majority of sections are by one Dominic DeSota or another, Pohl uses two other characters to add their first-person voices to the story: Larry Douglas narrates one section, and several different Nyla Christophes narrate several others. The main action of the novel takes place over several weeks in August 1983 and concludes in October 1983; Pohl dates each section and gives the full name and title of the person narrating the section.

Pohl intersperses very brief third-person sections with the first-person sections. These italicized paragraphs tell stories about places where the fabric between two parallel worlds has ruptured, allowing brief intersections between two parallel worlds. These sections remind me of sections of Leinster's "Sidewise in Time," which tell similar stories during the time quake that ruptures the world. These vignettes evoke alien but recognizable versions of Earth. In one section, a completely different Dom walks a trapline and catches an angora cat, formerly a pet, now dinner. In another, an old man runs to the mailbox to get his welfare check; when he returns a minute later, his apartment has been ransacked. He has been robbed. On his bed lies a man with a cut throat—himself. Later sections show behind-the-scenes action that relates to the plot of the novel as various people in various parallel time lines are kidnapped and taken to a detention center. Each of these sections tells the story of an individual, and each section merely hints at the world the individual is from and the nature of the parallel world that intersects with the character's reality.

Though each section advances the story, the reader must sort through a variety of doubled, tripled, quadrupled, and so on characters and an equally large number of worlds, keeping track of the nature of the world the character comes from, each character's rank, and the goal of each time line until the end, when the characters end up in the same detention area. Pohl sets forth a number of stories told in parallel, each moving from past to present to future. This narrative structure approximates the worlds themselves: simultaneous, yet moving forward. Pohl shows how environment affects the individual: Nyla Christophe can be a famed violinist and a thumbless sadist. One Dominic tells one Nyla: "In a way, we *did* have to be what we were, because of the world we lived in. 'Have to' might be too strong, because some of it was our fault—we took easy ways. There were better ways, even in our own time. But it wasn't all our fault, and we could have been a lot better" (292).

With this statement, Dominic foregrounds the notion of agency, the ability to act. With access to parallel worlds, Dominic knows exactly what he could have been: a senator or a physicist, among other things. Blaming how they turned out on their environment is too simple. Each person must make choices. Dominic goes on to say: "We could have been like them! And we still can be" (292). Pohl concludes with the characters' rebuilding an empty Earth, and rebuilding their lives along with it. This new parallel world provides everyone with new opportunities, new chances to act, but together this time instead of in parallel.

Piper and Pohl both foreground the ability of the individual to perform meaningful actions. Indeed, the parallel worlds story foregrounds this as well, as any action can result in the literal creation of multiple worlds. Parallel worlds writers take the quantum event that theoretically might result in fissioning worlds to a macroscopic level. Focusing on actions implicitly implies a focus on causes. But in parallel worlds stories, a single cause can result in an infinite number of effects—every effect possible. Parallel worlds thus focus on the model of history that concerns itself with the genesis of events. The Paratime stories have people who are able to create history from an event: they have cross-time line observers trained in history and other disciplines. In *Lord Kalvan*, Paratime historians study Kalvan because Kalvan finds himself transported to a world where he is able to generate significant effects by manipulating or creating causal events.

Simply knowing the recipe for gunpowder affects his new world profoundly; he topples the existing power structure and constructs a new one as the Paratimers observe eagerly, watching effects flow from the causes he brings about, using nearby time lines as controls. In "Last Enemy," Dalla uncovers a new procedure that allows consciousness to range over several lifetimes, in effect extending a person's life four- or fivefold. Here, cause and effect can be manipulated by an individual even after death, as discarnate entities have the power to reincarnate or not.

Similarly, Pohl's text focuses on the genesis of events. As the cats interact with one another, they learn of the lives that could have been theirs in a different environment with a different history. They learn that they have to take responsibility for their actions even as a superior time line removes them from their familiar worlds and puts them in a new one. Parallel worlds stories focus on the genesis of the event as brought about via agency. They point out that any person has the ability to create new universes through the slightest act. This gives tremendous power to the individual.

4 | Narrative, Temporality, and Historicity in Philip K. Dick's *The Man in the High Castle*

> Work the sentences, if you wish, so that they will mean something. . . .
> Or so that they mean nothing. Whichever you prefer.
> —Mr. Tagomi, *High Castle*

Chapters 2 and 3 rely on events-based cause-and-effect nexus points. Ward Moore's *Bring the Jubilee* (1955), the focus of chapter 2, has as a nexus point the Confederates' winning the Civil War, an outcome that occurred from a single but significant chance encounter. Chapter 3 focuses on simultaneous, parallel alternate worlds as articulated in H. Beam Piper's Paratime works and Frederik Pohl's *The Coming of the Quantum Cats* (1986). These texts focus on the infinite number of causes that literally bring about every possible outcome. Both of these chapters are based on the premise that events bring about effects, which is why I say they are both concerned with the genetic theory of history, which is concerned with the origin of something.

This chapter also uses the genetic model of history as its base. However, instead of actions—either significant, as in *Jubilee*, or insignificant, as in *Quantum Cats*—Philip K. Dick's *The Man in the High Castle* (1962) relies not on events but on the individual construction of reality. Dick sees the world as a reflection of the mind, not as something that results from historical forces.

High Castle—the novel widely regarded as Dick's greatest work—is a true alternate history, the term I use to refer to those texts that deal with the ramifications of a changed historical event years after the nexus event itself. Dick's novel takes place following the Japanese occupation of part of America after the Nazis win World War II. *High Castle* shifts the primary field of care from the future to the present and the past by estranging events and by using certain themes, notably art. Using Paul Ricoeur's arguments about time and repetition and applying them to *High Castle*, I argue that this text requires a rupture, a break that means we cannot rely on memory to allow time to be mediated through repetition. By conceiving of the world as something constructed by an individual mind, Dick throws the notions of reality and history into flux.

The narrative strategy Dick uses for *High Castle* is characteristically complex. Dick often uses a roving point of view in his novels. Many of Dick's novels are not a single person's story as much as an interweaving of stories that must be taken together, which results in narratively interesting play. Dick jumps around in space and (sometimes) time, and he never allows the reader to sympathize with any one protagonist. In a foreword to an interview with Dick that Paul Williams conducted on October 30, 1974, Williams notes that Dick modeled this characteristic narrative structure on "the multicharactered realistic novels produced by students in the French department of Tokyo University after World War II" (73). Dick tells Williams that he never liked the notion of a single protagonist because it did not reflect his understanding of the world. Dick prefers an articulation of the world that allows people to be linked:

> I really think that maybe the first responsibility of the novelist, as I conceive it, is to show this. He starts with a character and surmounts the view the individual reader has that he is a world unto himself, nobody else shares his problems and he doesn't share theirs.
>
> Then switch to another character and show some involvement. . . . the real thrill of the writing is to work through sixty thousand words without a preconception as to how these characters are linked. (Williams, 74–75)

The novel's narrative structure literalizes this kind of interweaving, an interweaving also used metaphorically in the *I Ching*, the use of which permeates the novel. To use the *I Ching*, the supplicant asks a question, throws a certain number of yarrow stalks or coins, and looks at the pattern they make. This is repeated six times. The patterns will fit hexagrams listed in the *I Ching*, each with a name or saying that gives guidance to the supplicant.

In fact, Dick used the *I Ching* to construct *High Castle* (Sutin, 112), just as Dick's novelist character Abendsen used it to write the alternate history inside the alternate history, *The Grasshopper Lies Heavy*, the banned book that the characters read furtively. These random relationships metaphorically "organize" the relationships between characters and the relationships between alternate times. Lawrence Sutin, Dick's biographer, notes that the "multiple viewpoints provide *High Castle* with a richness of texture that encompasses even the most subtle emotional shifts of its characters. The novel demonstrates convincingly that our smallest circumstantial acts can affect our fellow humans—for good or ill—more than we can ever likely know" (114). This point is well taken, as the genre of the alternate history argues much the same thing: change an event in history and see what results. This also links *High Castle* to the parallel worlds story, which allows each minor event to create a new and literal reality. Dick prefers the human, personal side of constructing reality to the models of reality that rely on quantum events.

The kind of linkage that Dick attempts to realize reveals itself in dislocation. The characters do not all know each other, but some characters know others, who in turn know others, creating a web of relationship. This kind of discontinuity, Susan Wells argues in an analysis of rhetoric, allows a representation of time that takes into account time as experienced:

> Temporal location enacts and renegotiates the positions of reader and writer. . . . The gaps and syncopations of narrative time and the demands that its contradictions make on readers bring to light what would otherwise be obscure: the discontinuity between time as a domain of subjective experience and time as the arena of force and motion. By performing this discontinuity in a text, narrative discourse permits us to see and understand what is unacknowledged in the representation of time as mechanical, uniform duration. (Wells, 51)

Because Dick wishes to focus on reality as an expression of an individual mind, his narrative must reinforce subjectivity over articulations of time as "mechanical" and "uniform." The discontinuity between the subjectivity of time and time as an arena of action is at issue in *High Castle*, which uses narrative to mediate between the self and action. *High Castle* tells the stories of a series of people experiencing time subjectively; the whole of the text moves outside the representation of time by cosmic cues (that is, by calendars, clocks, or other ways of representing or symbolizing time) and instead moves to an internal time sense. Ricoeur and others have argued, as Wells does above, that literature uses narrativity to mediate between subjective and cosmic time. There are two points of view that work together here: cosmic time moves alongside the individual's time sense.

However, *High Castle* uses its complex narrative structure to imply that subjective time and cosmic time are in fact the same thing, as the former creates the latter. Human agency and the subjective time sense are thus placed above an uncontrollable but regular cosmic time. Instead, the creation of *The Grasshopper Lies Heavy* by use of the *I Ching*, which implies some ordering system, however uncontrollable and random, takes the place of cosmic time.

The alternate history is a text placed at the crux of temporality, narrativity, and history; these three points engage in a dialogue that, in most alternate histories, question these topics by estranging them, by changing events or interpretations to make them unfamiliar. Ricoeur argues that analyzing narrative and temporality together bears out Heidegger's threefold view of time by pulling apart the notion of linear time. Using Heidegger, Ricoeur, in "Narrative Time," argues there are three constitutions of time (the threefold view of time). Heidegger's second constitution, that of historicality, is the one of interest here. In historicality, an emphasis is placed on the past to recover events through memory and thereby through repetition. *High Castle* places an emphasis on historicality and the past by making big business of the buying and selling of artifacts, including fake artifacts representing real ones.

Ricoeur argues (via Heidegger) that "the primary direction of care is toward the future," and therefore concerns about history, which are rooted in the past, are mediated through repetition, which unites future, past, and present ("Narrative Time," 182–83). David Farrell Krell, in his introduction to a Heidegger essay, notes in a translator's remark that Heidegger's use of the word "repetition" connotes "the sense of fetching something back as a new beginning," concluding that perhaps a better word choice might be "retrieval" or "reprise" (Krell, 42n). Indeed, Ricoeur parenthetically indicates that repetition is meant to mean "recapitulation" ("Narrative Time," 76). Although "repetition" is used throughout this essay in this specialized sense, it is just as easy to think of repetition as simply doing something again, as I believe the specialized sense of this word as expressed by philosophical scholars such as Krell, Heidegger, and Ricoeur implies that repetition is more complex than it really is.

Ricoeur, summarizing the notion of repetition, notes that repetition seeks "to recover the primacy of anticipatory resoluteness at the very heart of what is abolished, over and done with, what is no longer. Repetition thus opens potentialities that went unnoticed, were aborted, or were repressed in the past" (*Time and Narrative*, 3:76). Thus, new histories may explore the history of women in seventeenth-century France—a retelling of previously articulated or newly researched events with a new focus that takes into account modern thought about the importance of women in history. This can likewise occur on a purely personal level as individuals, through memory, make meaning of events.

Dick himself has written about his views on time. In an untitled essay published in the anthology *Science Fiction at Large*[1] (an essay that does not focus specifically on *High Castle*), Dick mentions his debt to (among others) Kant and Henri Bergson, the philosopher who argued that memory and consciousness were required for humanity's notion of time sense, not calendars or other measuring devices. Dick, using the metaphors of time as arrow and time as cycle, writes of St. Paul's famous metaphor of seeing the world as a reflection. Dick argues that Paul was saying we should see the universe backward:

"To see the universe backwards?" What would that mean? Well, let me give you one possibility: that we experience time backwards; or more precisely, that our inner subjective category of experience of time (in the sense which Kant spoke of, a way by which we arrange experience), our time experience is orthogonal to the flow of time itself—at right angles. . . . By experiencing time as we do, orthogonally to its actual direction, we get a totally wrong idea of the sequence of events, of causality, of what is past and what is future, where the universe is going. (Dick, Untitled, 206)

This notion of time sense is particularly interesting when considered in conjunction with *High Castle*: the characters in the novel see the universe orthogonally, but the novel also forces us, in the "real" world, to see the world similarly. Dick's desire to express time at right angles and to fully show the web of relationship that links people results in the novel's narrative structure.

Ricoeur's argument is useful because *High Castle* requires a rupture, a break that means we cannot rely on memory to allow us to mediate time through repetition. Indeed, memory is crucial to the entire notion of repetition, though some writers have posited kinds of human experience other than memory to engage in repetition, most notably the senses of taste, hearing, or smell. A snatch of a song, the smell of roasting turkey, and the taste of fresh raspberries may all trigger experiences of recapitulation, as authors from Proust to Faulkner to Porter have reminded us. For the retarded Benjy in William Faulkner's *The Sound and the Fury* (1929), for example, hearing a word (*caddie*) is enough to cause him to relive an experience he associates with that word (*Caddy*, his sister). Time and space are meaningless to Benjy—and to the reader, who must sort through clues in Benjy's environment to figure out where and when Benjy is. Benjy seems to experience each event as new. He cannot contextualize the things that happen to him, so he has no sense of past, present, or future. He has memories, but no thought to go with these memories that will place the events in his life into a context (the opposite of his brother Quentin, who is acutely aware of context). Benjy, unable to engage meaningfully in repetition, is doomed to live always in the present.

Alternate histories work by dissociating the text from repetition, which means that memory does not help us make sense of events. This is true for both the reader of *High Castle* and for the characters within it. Alternate histories play with history, saying that things we know to be true are not true. Because everyone relies on the past to make sense of the present, when the past is changed, the present may be treacherous to negotiate. Unlike the characters in most alternate histories, who tend to live as unquestioningly in their world as we live in ours, the characters in *High Castle* find that repetition is problematic. This is expressed both literally and symbolically, as my discussion below outlines. The readers of the novel already find their memories useless in terms of contextualizing the alternate world, as Dick has negated the role of memory that alternate histories play with.

Changing the outcome of events means our memories about these events will not be reinforced. Instead of repetition, there is something new. Though *High Castle* takes place in an America where the Japanese have occupied part of the United States after World War II, and therefore refers to a past we can explain, the focus of the text's story, themes, and structure negates the role of memory and repetition. Instead of looking to the future, we look to the present and to the past—to the present to collate breaks with our present and to the past to find the rupture that caused the breaks. Ricoeur and Heidegger assert that ultimately, all narrativity leads toward death, the final, future event. In the alternate history, and in *High Castle*, the primary field of care is shifted in order to modify the notion of repetition by changing historical signifiers. The history in alternate histories relies on outcomes different from authentic historical outcomes. This results in repetition that serves not as a reassessment of the past but as a refiguring. Indeed, Dick refigures our history yet again in *The Grasshopper Lies Heavy*. Like *High Castle*, *Grasshopper* is an alternate history, one that creates a world in which the Nazis lost World War II. However, it is as different from our world as is the world of *High Castle*. *Grasshopper* posits an end to the color divide between black and white after 1950, rocket ships, China under democratic Chiang Kai-shek ushering in a "Decade of Rebuilding," and the United States' sending cheap television sets to Africa and Asia (150–54).

One metaphor for this shift of care to the past is Dick's use of American artifacts. In Dick's alternate world, Japanese collectors love Americana, and a brisk market has grown up around the buying and selling of these products. Robert Childan owns American Artistic Handcrafts Inc., which caters to the upwardly mobile Japanese market, specializing in "priceless antique artifacts from the pages of American history. Alas, all too rapidly vanishing into limbo of time" (*High Castle*, 51). Childan sells Mickey Mouse watches, weapons, posters, and the like, remnants of American popular culture before the Japanese occupation. In addition to selling originals, Childan also sells fakes, though of course he does not know it. A black market that creates and sells forgeries of these art objects has sprung up. The forgers replicate and repeat the past, but the replication is purposeless, because bits of the past are removed from their context. Some collectors have no idea what the objects they purchase are for. Childan, for instance, points out to someone that the "Horrors of War" gum cards were used as flip cards in a game he played when he was a boy. In other words, Japanese collectors attempt to evoke the American past without linking it meaningfully to the past. They cannot engage in repetition to order meaning because they are of a different milieu.

The Japanese living in America and the tradesmen who meet their needs want authenticity. They wish to own a piece of the past that existed while that past existed. They wish to have a piece of past in the present. Fake artifacts, such as the gun Childan has appraised, only to discover it is a clever copy, link the present and the past in that something is made in the present in order to evoke the past. This parallels the characters' interest in owning, but not necessarily understanding, the past. Japanese investors desire the history that goes along with the object; however, the history is not implicitly present in the object but constructed by the beholder, often using input learned from another source, such as Childan's childhood memories. Dick calls the aura of authenticity that surrounds an object "historicity":

> "Don't you feel it?" [Wyndam-Matson] kidded her [Rita]. "The historicity?"
> She said, "What is 'historicity'?"
> "When a thing has history in it. Listen. One of those two Zippo lighters was in Franklin D. Roosevelt's pocket when he was assassinated. And one wasn't. One has historicity, a hell of a lot of it. As much as any object ever had. And one has nothing. Can you feel it?" He nudged her. "You can't. You can't tell which is which. There's no 'mystical plasmic presence,' no 'aura' around it."
> . . . "It's in here." He tapped his head. "In the mind, not the [object]." (*High Castle*, 59)

George Slusser condenses Wyndam-Matson's point as this: historicity is "the desire for a particular relationship between the individual and the historical act" (203). I like this idea. Those who purchase Childan's objects (including Wyndam-Matson's fake revolvers) desire a personal connection with history. (Readers are expected to know that in our history, Franklin Roosevelt was not assassinated. The object is supposed to give meaning and authenticity to a certain set of historical events which, for us, did not happen.) The focus on the past here—on the altered past—and its attendant concerns about authenticity and its creation within the individual are used by the reader to document the world Dick has created. Dick's Japanese-occupied America, although discontinuous with reality, is still based on a history we recognize.

Earlier, I noted that Ricoeur's use of the word "repetition" actually connoted a reprise or a recapitulation. Dick, by writing an alternate history, actively seeks to avoid this notion of repetition. Though art objects are faked, though the history is our past as well as the past of Dick's world, the result is the characters' present: a present where Africans have been wiped out altogether, where slavery exists in San Francisco, and where rocket ships will soon land on Mars. The pasts may be shared up to the nexus point, but the present has become new. For the reader, memory and repetition are invalidated (not as processes but in specifics) in *High Castle* because the text is an alternate history discontinuous with the reader's reality; and because of the multiple interpretations offered for the same events.

Though much of the novel focuses on objects that represent the past, Dick does contemplate the new. The primary metaphor Dick uses when doing so is art. Two examples of this suffice. The first is the banned book, *The Grasshopper Lies Heavy*, itself an alternate history, which creates something new out of the past, again shifting the concept of time from the future to the past and the (new) present. This book, which many of the book's characters read with interest, posits a world where the Nazis lost World War II. But the world its author, Hawthorne Abendsen, creates is not our world but another one altogether. Juliana comes to realize the role of chance in constituting time. Abendsen wrote the book by casting coins and consulting the *I Ching*. While facing down Abendsen, Juliana asks the oracle, "Oracle, why did you write *The Grasshopper Lies Heavy*? What are we supposed to learn?" (246). The response is Chung Fu, Inner Truth. Abendsen responds angrily, "It means, does it, that my book is true?" and Juliana assents (247). Abendsen and Juliana's world is thus not true—and neither is ours, for the events in *Grasshopper* differ from what we know to be true. Is our world, then, an alternate history? Dick, as usual, does not tell us. For him, reality is the central question, never the answer to a question. But the hexagram consulted makes another point to the careful reader of *High Castle*: truth (and history) is created inside the individual. Inner Truth indeed.

The second example that shows Dick focusing on the present rather than the future is the jewelry Frank Frick and his partner display at Childan's shop. This handmade modern jewelry lacks historicity and a past. Childan gives some pieces to a Japanese customer, who believes these new pieces have *wu*, or an authenticity within themselves. Childan dimly remembers that *wu* has something to do with wisdom; critic Patricia Warrick defines *wu* as "letting things work out their destinies in accord with their intrinsic principles. Opposing *wu* is the concept of *wei*, forcing things in the interests of private gain, without regard to their intrinsic principles and relying on the authority of others" (50).

The piece of jewelry containing *wu* is quite different from the other objects Childan sells, which focus on evoking authenticity by eliciting a response from the person looking at the artwork. The viewer is prompted to create authenticity by relying on the assurances of people like Childan that the object is authentic and historic; sometimes, a piece of paper proclaims authenticity. The objects containing *wu* are different because they are products of the present. Childan turns down the chance to make a tremendous amount of money by mass-producing the metallic squiggles. Mass production would not be true to the *wu* within the object itself, which requires uniqueness. Such an exploitation would mean the *wu*-filled objects would become *wei*, which implies private profit. In addition, endless duplication of this sort of unique object would violate what Warrick calls "intrinsic principles."

The fake guns Wyndham-Mason's company makes are another permutation of *wei*. Childan shows the jewelry with *wu* to Mr. Tagomi, saying: "These are not the old. . . . Sir, these are the new. . . . This is the new life of my country, sir. The beginning in the form of tiny imperishable seeds. Of beauty" (215–16). This hints at a future, but Dick does not allow this idea to grow, content to let it remain a small, metallic seed. The authenticity of the jewelry with *wu* lies in the pieces' lack of historicity. The Zippo lighter in FDR's pocket when he was assassinated gains status as an object containing historicity because it is linked to a past event (assuming the Zippo is not another elaborate fake). The jewelry with *wu* has historicity because of the pieces' intrinsic quality; as John Huntington notes, "the value of the artifact with *wu* exists absolutely and needs no certification" (175). *Wu* is a constant. History and historicity are not.

High Castle further problematizes history and historicity by foregrounding the theme of chance, the *I Ching* used by Abendsen to write *The Grasshopper Lies Heavy* (and by Dick himself when writing *High Castle*). The glimpses we as readers see of the world of *Grasshopper* are tantalizing; we naturally want to know if it is our world, the "real" world, that is described within, only to discover that it is not. The *I Ching* implies that we must add our world to the pile of alternate worlds. The *I Ching*'s role is not to tell the future or to tell the present—there is no sense of mystic certainty here—but to give the supplicant tools for negotiating these things by providing insight. There is no point in providing our world as *High Castle*'s alternate world; there would be nothing to learn here and it would defy Dick's themes of estrangement and reality. The readers of *Grasshopper* read it for the same reason that we read *High Castle*.

In a different context, David Wood writes, "The *I Ching*, the book of changes, teaches us to recognize intelligible patterns of change, and that time is a condition for these patterns and not a threat to them" (335). Dick attempts to construct, by use of the alternate history, an intelligible pattern of change; the character who understands this is Tagomi.

Tagomi shifts briefly into "our" San Francisco after closely observing a piece of the jewelry with *wu*. He thinks: "seen through glass darkly not a metaphor, but astute reference to optical distortion . . . our space and our time creations of our own psyche" (224). (Remember that Dick uses St. Paul to prove that time is orthogonal.) Moments like this, inspired by an object, lead John Rieder to argue that "the structure of *High Castle*'s world can best be understood not as an alternative history constructed by reversing the roles of conquerors and conquered in World War II, but rather as a complex set of metafictional possibilities concretized by objects and texts within the novel" (226). *High Castle*'s purpose is, as Rieder suggests, to make concrete, through artifacts and through the characters and their minds, these "metafictional possibilities" by failing to distinguish between the real and the artificial and by failing to grant one interpretation ascendancy. However, the status of the novel as an alternate history bears the same amount of importance as the artifacts; dismissing the genre is too easy. I argue that it has the same status as do the objects and texts Rieder discusses. The point is not to "[reverse] the roles of conquerors and conquered in World War II" but to cause us to realize that (in Tagomi's words) "we list eccentrically, all sense of balance gone" (Rieder, 224). The status of the novel as an alternate history, the faked objects (the guns), and the new objects (the jewelry) force us to view the world differently, because memory cannot be used to negotiate Dick's created world—not for us, the readers, and not for the novel's characters. Instead, memory causes us to call into question Dick's world and the world we each construct that we call reality.

Both Juliana and Tagomi realize that the world is constituted not by a linear series of nows, the nows that make up so much of our thinking when we think of time, but by the individual. Tagomi realizes this by contemplating *wu*; Juliana realizes this when she meets Abendsen and discovers he used the oracle and chance to write *The Grasshopper Lies Heavy*. Indeed, there are several links between Juliana and the jewelry with *wu*. Juliana and the jewelry are both (as Mrs. Abendsen says of Juliana) "terribly, terribly disruptive"; Mr. Abendsen's response is, "So is reality" (248). Like the jewelry, Juliana is a force of *wu*: "She's doing what is instinctive to her, simply expressing her being" (247), resulting in disarray. Dick parallels this disarray with the disruption of history and time. History, time, and space, however, are not objective truths but, as Tagomi realizes, the product of the human mind. Ricoeur's repetition (a reprise, a retrieval), used to organize and make meaning out of events, results in a retelling of events from a new point of view. Dick reverses this: the point of view will determine the events.

Dick's reversal, which relies on *wu* and on an individual in order to make meaning, refutes Ricoeur's argument that in fiction, historical events escape having to stand for something:

> From the mere fact that the narrator and the leading characters are fictional, all references to real historical events are divested of their function of standing for the historical past and are set on a par with the unreal status of the other events. . . . Historical events are no longer denoted, they are simply mentioned. . . . The entire range of tools serving the relation of standing-for can be fictionalized in this way and considered as the work of the imaginary. (Ricoeur, *Time and Narrative*, 3:129)

For Dick, however, historical and ahistorical events do more than create a backdrop for the action of the text. The themes of chance, historicity, and authenticity work back around to the theme of the imaginary versus the real. As Tagomi remarks, individuals create time and space, and thus history exists only as construction.

Though *High Castle* rethinks history first by altering it from our own and second by not allowing the characters to make history through repetition, *High Castle* does use repetition narratively by linking it to structure. Repetition is used literally, complete with rearticulations and reassessments of events that occur within the text. This repetition serves to further fragment the narrative by again foregrounding the place of the individual in making meaning of an event. Dick's narrative structure results in an articulation of a number of different experiences, some alluded to more than once, allowing for repetition and thus reinterpretation of an event. This repetition or recapitulation does not occur through characters' memories but through events.

Though Dick sometimes reassesses an event in a word or two by having a character briefly remember an experience, one event Dick describes twice in *High Castle* is Juliana's murder of Joe Cinnadella, whom she discovers wants to kill Abendsen. Dick describes the murder itself and then repeats it when Juliana, a former martial arts instructor, reads about it in the newspaper. The actual murder is surprisingly oblique, in part because of Juliana's fragile mental state:

> Whisk. "It is awful," she said. "They violate. I ought to know." Ready for purse snatcher; the various night prowlers, I can certainly handle.

Where had this one gone? Slapping his neck, doing a dance. "Let me by," she said. . . .

Still sitting on the floor, clasping the side of his neck, Joe said, "Listen. You're very good. You cut my aorta. Artery in my neck."

Giggling, she clapped her hand to her mouth. "Oh God—you're such a freak. I mean, you get words all wrong. The aorta's in your chest; you mean the carotid."

"If I let go," he said, "I'll bleed out in two minutes." (204–5)

Juliana's disconnection from the scene; her leaving the room, only to be sent back by a maid because she is nude; and her forgetting to tell someone about Joe's condition muffle any sense of upset or urgency, indicating Juliana's emotional distance from her act. Dick maintains this tone by using a newspaper article to revisit the hotel room where Juliana left Joe holding his cut throat: "Sought for questioning concerning the fatal slashing of her husband in their swank rooms at the President Garner Hotel in Denver, Mrs. Joe Cinnadella of Canon City, according to hotel employees, left immediately after what must have been the tragic climax of a marital quarrel. . . . The hotel suite, police said, showed signs of a struggle, suggesting that a violent argument had . . ." (237).

Dick cuts off the retelling midsentence, but the revisitation of the event results in a faulty translation, an incorrect interpretation. It is, perhaps, no more incorrect than Abendsen's interpretation of events that occur after the Nazis lose World War II in *The Grasshopper Lies Heavy*. Events occur and characters imbue them with meaning. Sometimes the meanings do not agree.

The narrativity in *High Castle* foregrounds the fact that meaningfulness is the result of the human mind, just as the notion of historicity lies in the human's capacity to find something important because it links the individual to the past. George Slusser argues that history and narrativity are intertwined in *High Castle*, noting that historicity "is a *process* of interaction between mind and matter. . . . it originates within the realm of narrative itself, and in doing so declares that realm a prime basis for activity. . . . [Story] becomes a prime mover in the relativistic temporal field I call historicity" (221). Story and time reverse their usual fields of care in this paradigm.

The theme of chance unifies these differing interpretations; or, perhaps, instead of unifying, it simply critiques. Dick does not like resolution. In her analysis of Dick's *High Castle*, Patricia S. Warrick notes that Dick likes to present a thesis and then, in a later work or perhaps within the same text, an antithesis: "Any system that comes to power represents a thesis. Because this thesis has been achieved, rebellion against it must begin—the antithesis must be asserted. . . . Once he has asserted an idea in a novel, he tends to follow it with a counterassertion in another novel" (37). For Dick, multiple interpretations of the same event are as possible as multiple events with the same interpretation. In *High Castle*, the thesis/antithesis is a Dickian joke: if the story is thesis, then our world is antithesis.

Ricoeur notes that "the invincible word . . . teaches [us] that we do not produce time but that it surrounds us, envelops us, and overpowers us with its awesome strength" (*Time and Narrative*, 3:17). Dick attempts to hold this invincibility at bay by writing a story that contains metaphors of control, no matter how tenuous. Dick and Abendsen throw the yarrow stalks; chance and the human mind construct a reality. Dick, whose works often focus on an individual or series of individuals struggling with the nature of reality, pushes aside space and time as external truisms and instead makes them a part of the human psyche. *High Castle*, as an alternate history, focuses attention on the past and its relation to the present, erasing (or covering) care for the future. Dick liberates time from a future-looking series of nows by implying that both the past and the present can move orthogonally as well as linearly, but that any such movement is a product of mind, not of time.

5 | Looking Forward: William Gibson and Bruce Sterling's *The Difference Engine*

> And yet the execution of the so-called Modus Program demonstrated that any formal system must be both *incomplete* and *unable to establish its own consistency*. There is no finite mathematical way to express the property of "truth." The *transfinite* nature of the Byron Conjectures were the ruination of the Grand Napoleon; the Modus Program initiated a series of nested loops, which, though difficult to establish, were yet more difficult to extinguish. The program ran, yet rendered its Engine useless!
>
> —Ada, *The Difference Engine*

Whereas the previous three chapters interested themselves in a model of history concerned with the cause in cause and effect, this chapter, which focuses on William Gibson and Bruce Sterling's *The Difference Engine* (1991), takes as its premise a model of history concerned with final causes. Teleological concerns are future oriented and concerned with design or purpose. All alternate histories concern themselves with cause and effect, as I have argued throughout this book. However, the point of a cause-and-effect structure is open to interpretation. Like Philip K. Dick's *The Man in the High Castle* (1962), *Difference* uses a narrative structure that links together disparate stories. Dick negotiates a web of relationships. Gibson and Sterling do the same, though on a longer time scale. Though Dick concludes that the human mind creates reality and history, Gibson and Sterling do not go this far, preferring the far more common tactic of assuming the reality of events. Gibson and Sterling use their unique narrative to mix the real and the unreal. Whereas Dick looks to causes, which he concludes lie in the individual, Gibson and Sterling look forward to a possible effect.

I focus on *Difference* because of its discursive loops of cause and effect, loops that iterate endlessly but that create something in their iteration. *Difference*, through its elliptical and odd narrative structure, foregrounds the randomness of events. In addition to an analysis of the novel's use of iteration, I discuss the strategies Gibson and Sterling use to structure the narrative of the novel, and I discuss the authors' choice of characters, some of whom are real historical figures and some of whom are invented.

In this discussion, I take as a given the connection between the linear notion of time and the notion of cause and effect. In texts that do not deal with time travel (see chapter 2 for a discussion of time-travel texts in relation to metaphors of time), this link is obvious: cause happens first and results in effect. The narrative structure of texts, also linear, explicitly links events into a cause-and-effect pattern, sometimes called a story or a plot. In chapter 4, I focused on the point Paul Ricoeur makes in *Time and Narrative* that narrative relies on repetition, arguing that Dick does not permit memory and repetition to work together to build history or reality.

In contrast, in this chapter, I discuss *Difference*'s use of repetition in terms of iteration, which *Webster's Tenth* defines as "a procedure in which repetition of a sequence of operations yields results successively closer to a desired result." *Difference* uses iteration in the computer programming sense, too; this kind of iteration will repeat computer instructions the number of times specified by the program or "until a condition is met." The iterations in *Difference* work to an end, though the end does not appear to be a condition set by the programmers. Instead, it is a logical outgrowth of technology. The concluding events in *Difference*, the creation of a new, computer-based artificial intelligence, as well as the too-early computer age (the premise of the nexus event), bring about an anticipatory text, one concerned with teleological concerns. Another term that might be used as a synonym for *teleological* is *design-oriented*. I link design to the iterations that literally make up the narrative structure.

In a review of *The Difference Engine*, Glenn Grant writes:

The Difference Engine is evolution, the generator of novelty, diversity, complexity. It exists because it exists. No reason, no purpose, no design, just the imperative — spelled out in patterns of proteins or neural nets or electrons or punch-cards — to replicate the pattern.

The Difference Engine is information. (37)

Grant's review reduces the novel to the barest bones of its theme: the endless replication and iteration of information. I cannot read Grant's words, however, without noticing that his comment may speak just as well to narrative. Narrative, which structures stories, replicates its pattern as we tell stories. It exists because we exist, and we imbue narrative with meaning.

Difference is a particularly rich text to discuss because its pattern links together truth and fiction. Indeed, the novel itself replicates the imperative of the pattern, as I will show below. The novel takes place in London in 1855, but in a London where Charles Babbage's prototype computer, the Difference Engine, actually worked. The nexus point in *Difference* is the successful creation of the Difference Engine, which Babbage — in our world — constructed in 1822 but was unable to improve upon because of the limitations of the mechanical pieces in responding to stress. The original Difference Engine was "an adding machine for the computation of polynomials, and worked to an accuracy of six decimal places" (E. Gunn, 44). *Difference* takes place in London some thirty years after the triumphant success of the Difference Engine.

In this alternate history, the elections of 1830 heralded a shift in the balance of power toward Byron and his Industrial Radical Party; they seized control in 1831 by fomenting a class war. In our history, *Radical* was a term used to refer to "all those who supported the movement for parliamentary reform" after 1797 (E. Gunn, 51). The upshot of all this change: in this alternate past, the aristocracy has become a meritocracy, with lordships granted for significant scientific discoveries. The world is changing quickly, with information technology available to many. Rationality rules. Young men — and even some women, such as Ada, Byron's daughter, nicknamed the Queen of the Engines — turn to "clacking" (what we would call "hacking") and other Engine programming. Gibson and Sterling write, "Babbage's very first Engine, now an honored relic, was still less than thirty years old, but the swift progression of Enginery had swept a whole generation in its wake, like some mighty locomotive of the mind" (131). The computer age has come to Britain a hundred years too early; Engines now permeate every part of life.

The plot revolves around two mysterious boxes of punch cards made to run on a French Engine gauge. (Engines store information by using punch cards such as those used to program Jacquard looms.) We are led to believe that the mysterious boxes contain a Modus, a program written by Ada that will be a foolproof gambling system. Ada gives the boxes containing the cards to Edward Mallory during a chance encounter; he hides them in the head of a dinosaur on exhibit at his place of employment, where they are stolen by persons unknown.

Meanwhile, part-time thief and prostitute Sybil Gerard witnesses a near-fatal attack on Sam Houston (who employs her boyfriend, Mick Radley) and flees to France, where, armed with diamonds she has stolen from Houston, she buys a new life and a new identity for herself. Laurence Oliphant puts all the pieces together. The cards were stolen from their hiding place and were then run on the French machine, the Great Napoleon, which rendered the Engine useless. Oliphant reconstructs the story after the fact and gives Sybil a chance to revenge herself upon her ex-lover, Charles Egremont, now an important person in British government.

The plot summary above only hints at the loops of text that link the characters. Gibson and Sterling divide the novel into five sections called "Iterations" and a concluding "Modus" (with the word *Modus* also used as the name of Ada's gambling system). These five chronological sections range forward in time, sometimes by many years. Each section focuses on a different character or a different event that sketches out actions referred to later in the novel. These actions are later contextualized by Oliphant. The purpose of this organization is to show the result of events outlined in the novel. Sybil Gerard, Edward Mallory, and Laurence Oliphant, the three main characters, encounter each other directly or indirectly through an odd set of circumstances. Gibson and Sterling play up the randomness of events and connections: Mallory, for example, purchases the services of a prostitute who used to be a friend of Sybil's; this prostitute now owns Sybil's cat. Mallory and Oliphant work together to find out who is stalking Mallory. Oliphant meets Sybil for the first time in Paris many years after the main action of the story. And Sybil and Sam Houston (the man she left for dead years ago when she stole his diamond cache) almost run into each other in Paris. The characters move and intersect—or fail to intersect—with one another.

The five Iterations work toward the final result, but the result does not have to do with the action of the novel but with the themes: the novel concludes with the creation of the All-Seeing Eye (reminiscent of Wintermute's change into a self-aware, powerful artificial intelligence in Gibson's

1984 cyberpunk novel *Neuromancer*), an artificial intelligence that has sprung from the Engine, what Gibson and Sterling call "a *thing* . . . an auto-catalytic tree, in almost-life, feeding through the roots of thought on the rich decay of its own shed images, and ramifying, through myriad lightning-branches, up, up toward the hidden light of vision" (429). Though the novel concludes with what we would consider an archaic technology spawning a sophisticated artificial intelligence—something that has eluded contemporary scientists so far—this intelligence is the culmination of the novel's theme of iteration. The birth of the All-Seeing Eye is the final effect of the Babbage machine in the 1991 of this alternate world.

The concluding Modus section is a microcosm of the structure of the five Iterations: it is made up of snippets of quotations, plays, poetry, depositions, and the like. Some of these texts were written by Gibson and Sterling. Some of them were not and are real historical artifacts. However, Gibson and Sterling do not reveal which is which. The reader must instead accord them all the same status, just as the reader must fit together the five Iterations with the Modus. Like Ada's gambling Modus, however, it reduces information to the written equivalent of the punch cards that drive an Engine. The Engine reads and interprets the coding held on the cards, then executes what it reads. The reader must read the Modus and attempt to link the random statements therein. The reader must act as the Engine and make meaning of the text, just as scientists examine data and draw conclusions from it.

Each Iteration begins with a moment frozen in time—a still life, a photograph, a frozen image from a surveillance device, an object—each capturing a moment, holding it, and then shifting it to the moment the artifact was created. Most of these moments occur later in time than the events of the novel do, making these objects historical artifacts, traces of events that have gone before. The first is a "composite image" of Sybil Gerard, taken in 1904, and shows her sitting on a balcony in France, resting "her arthritic hands upon fabric woven by a Jacquard loom." Gibson and Sterling link the complexity of weaving to the complexity of Sybil herself: "These hands consist of tendons, tissue, jointed bone. Through quiet processes of time and information, threads within the human cells have woven themselves into a woman" (1). The punch cards of the Jacquard loom evoke the punch cards of the Engine as well as human biology and its attendant replication of DNA, all coding and reiterating information. These moments provide a historical frame as the objects evoke the past—the story's present. But even as they evoke the past, Gibson and

Sterling imply an alternate present as well: behind Sybil fly "tiny unmanned aeroplanes," and she sees an airship and its lights (2). The objects that seek to make history from historical artifacts are themselves from a context that we do not understand. Gibson and Sterling estrange both the past and the present in *Difference*.

The randomness of the images that begin each Iteration complements the randomness that still manages to bring three people into the same time and space. With this is linked, in turn, the characters themselves: Gibson and Sterling mix their characters with real people and other authors' literary creations. Sybil Gerard, along with other characters in her section of the book, including her lover Mick Radley, her father Walter Gerard, and her ex-lover Charles Egremont, are characters in the Benjamin Disraeli novel *Sybil, or The Two Nations*, a popular book about class warfare published in 1845. The characters in *Difference*, however, have been twisted. In Disraeli's novel, the beautiful, virginal Sybil (she is expected to take orders and become a nun) and the rich and charming Charles Egremont, M.P., end up together. In Disraeli's novel, Dandy Mick is a sixteen-year-old waif. *Sybil*, which along with two other books form what is known as Disraeli's "Young England" trilogy (Butler, 9), contrasts the vapid life of the rich—one of the characters actually says, "I feel so cursed blasé!" (26)—with the desperate poverty of the working classes and the poor. R. A. Butler, in his introduction to *Sybil*, notes that the text is more political tract than novel (11).

In *Difference*, Gibson and Sterling ask, "What would have happened if the characters in Disraeli's novel had been affected by the computer age?" In *Difference*, Sybil bore Charles's child out of wedlock after he abandoned her; she has become a fallen woman and he has become prominent in government, a Member of Parliament like Disraeli's Egremont. Charles plays a large role in *Sybil* but hardly appears in *Difference*, where Gibson and Sterling only allude to him. And Dandy Mick, who is sixteen in Disraeli's novel, is Sybil's current (and older) lover in *Difference*. He works for Sam Houston, who is attempting to win back some of the political power he has lost as ex-president of Texas. *Difference*'s Dandy Mick is an expert clacker, or Engine programmer.

Disraeli is not the only Victorian author Gibson and Sterling borrow. In an interview conducted in Toronto in April 1991, while Gibson and Sterling were on a tour promoting *Difference*, Gibson and Sterling note that hardly any prominent Victorian author remained unscathed. Gibson calls this technique "literary sampling":

I think we applied word-processing technology to a traditional process of plagiarism and did something really new because a great deal of the intimate texture of this book derives from the fact that it's an enormous collage of little pieces of forgotten Victorian textual material which we lifted from Victorian journalism, from Victorian pulp literature. We lifted a lot of sensation novels, particularly the novels of Mary Braddon, who wrote . . . *Lady Audley's Secret.* There are pieces of *Lady Audley's Secret* embedded brazenly in our text. Virtually all of the interior descriptions, the descriptions of furnishings, are simply descriptive sections lifted from Victorian literature. Then we worked it, we sort of air-brushed it with the word-processor, we bent it slightly, and brought out eerie blue notes that the original writers could not have. It's sort of like Jimi Hendrix playing "The Star-Spangled Banner." (Fischlin, Hollinger, and Taylor, 9)

Sterling goes on to say that after copying text directly from the original, the two of them would rewrite it, along with the invented sections, swapping floppy disks back and forth, until the lifted text merged with the invented text.

In addition to the characters pulled from Disraeli and Braddon, Gibson and Sterling use as characters people who actually existed. Edward "Leviathan" Mallory, who in the novel is a paleontologist, the discoverer of the Brontosaurus, and a sometime gunrunner in Wyoming, was in real life a New England hatmaker notable chiefly because he lived to be 117 (E. Gunn, 48), a fate Gibson and Sterling play with. Mallory, the son of a Sussex hatmaker, exclaims to another character, speaking of the vagaries of history, "'History'! You think you should have a title and estates and I should rot in Lewes making hats" (301).

Laurence Oliphant is also a historical figure, though a rather more famous one, a writer of travel books and, perhaps, a spy. In the novel, he covers up his spy activities by writing books about his travels, thereby convincing people he is primarily a writer—a tactic the real Oliphant, if he was in fact a spy, is thought to have done. Also like his real-life counterpart, he suffers from syphilis. Other minor characters step in from the history books as well: John Keats, a clacker, appears very briefly; Byron is mentioned as an important political figure; Wilkie Collins is Captain Swing; and Ada Byron, who loves to gamble, appears once in a drugged haze and again as a lecturer in France. "Dizzy" Disraeli himself appears in a cameo as he attempts to learn how to work a typewriting machine that takes dictation. Gibson and Sterling present all these characters without any indication of who is real, who is their invention, and who is invention by way of another author.

The Victorian age is recognizable, though there is much of our own machine-age world and information age in it as well. In fact, Paul Alkon notes that *Difference* is a novel about our own time as much as it is a fantasy about a time that will never be. In his analysis of the alternate history as postmodern discourse, Alkon argues that *Difference* playfully subverts twentieth-century technological innovations: "Gibson and Sterling create the impression that had Babbage succeeded the world would simply have resembled ours a little sooner though dressed in fashions of the previous season." Alkon argues that the text is "very much of a piece with postmodern modes of abolishing historicity by denying essential differences between chronologically disparate times" ("Alternate History," 80, 81).

Though Gibson and Sterling painstakingly researched the novel—they began writing it in 1983—and incorporated touches of Victoriana throughout the text, they extrapolate the Victorian forward, showing how the Engine affects identity, fashion, leisure, and politics. Indeed, I find Frank Kermode's notion of *temporal integration* useful here. Kermode defines this term as "our way of bundling together perception of the present, memory of the past, and expectation of the future in a common organization" (46). *Difference* asks the reader to integrate the events in the story with reality by examining and querying the nature of cause and effect. Alkon argues that the structure of cause and effect that Gibson and Sterling construct ultimately fails because the past as expressed in the novel and our present are too close, thereby destroying historicity by failing to differentiate between times. Although I certainly agree that Gibson and Sterling destroy historicity, I would argue that Gibson and Sterling play with the notion of integration, with the *constructedness* of cause and effect, which they foreground with techniques that focus on iteration. Their narrative play (and their plays on words and plays on technological innovations that are old news to the modern reader) allows free play of cause and effect.

Indeed, we see characters struggling with their perceptions in order to make sense of what they see. Edward "Leviathan" Mallory, in his old age and with two major triumphs behind him—the discovery of the Brontosaur and the articulation of the theory of continental drift—is faced with two folders. Gibson and Sterling show him making a choice; if he opens the one on the left, he grows so upset that an artery collapses and he dies. "That chain of events does not occur," Gibson and Sterling tell us (321), foregrounding the pattern, tossing aside one possibility after having drawn it to its conclusion. Instead, he turns to the folder on the right, a field report from Canada. He looks at several pictures of bizarre, soft-bodied creatures; one "is a legless, ray-like thing, all lobes and jelly, with a flat, fanged mouth that does not bite but irises shut. . . . These things bear no relation to any known creature, from any known period whatever." At that moment, Mallory experiences an epiphany, a sudden, clear understanding as he begins to sort through data and reach a conclusion; he feels "an ecstatic rush toward utter comprehension" as he suddenly fits it all together. Then he dies, and with him "a knowledge that is dying to be born" (322).

The outcomes of these two scenarios are the same: either way, Leviathan Mallory's time has come. He dies. But one of his choices allows him to die with meaning, just as he has distinguished himself by, Engine-like, fitting together bits of information to draw a conclusion. He must make sense of the bizarre soft-bodied fossils that face him just before his moment of death, just as he made sense of the quick-moving but cold-blooded dinosaurs whose bones he hunted in the wilds of Wyoming. Mallory, as a paleontologist, finds fossils—an effect—from which he constructs a cause. Likewise, we make sense of *Difference* by putting together the five Iterations and the Modus and constructing a cause from the provided effect. In mixing truth and fiction, Gibson and Sterling destroy historicity and foreground the constructedness of cause and effect.

Paul Ricoeur notes that texts that anticipate the future might also be profitably thought of as "anticipated retrospections," because narrative can be anywhere in time the writer desires. Indeed, this phrase is particularly apt, considering the framework of the novel, with each Iteration beginning with a frozen event in the future looking back at the past. But for the reader, this narrated time becomes the "quasi-present." Ricoeur notes that prophecy and utopia are two ways of articulating this. The former sees the present moving "toward its future ruin as something that has already happened." The latter sees the present as moving to a utopian ideal. He concludes, "So the future seems to be representable only given the assistance of anticipatory narratives that transform a living present into a future perfect mode—this present will have been the beginning of a history that will one day be told" (Ricoeur, *Time and Narrative*, 3:260). Hayden White articulates similar ideas in *Metahistory* when he discusses, via Karl Mannheim, four ideological positions, any one of which a historian might take. The ideological position closest to *Difference* is Radicalism, when a utopian condition is immanent, a future-looking mode.

Gibson and Sterling write an "anticipated retrospection" in *Difference*. It builds a quasi-present in the nineteenth century, but one recognizable to us because we understand computers. The clockwork machines of *Difference* are not too different from our silicon-based technology, and the characters seem to use their version of computers in much the same way we use ours: mass production, fashion, advertisements, visual aids for speeches, tracking people, printing, and so on. This aspect of the novel has led to criticism that the authors were not imaginative enough to divorce the clockwork Engine world from our microprocessor-based computer world.

However, the important difference, and one that, to use Ricoeur's words, "transform[s] a living present into a future perfect mode," is the All-Seeing Eye, the artificial intelligence that springs from the iterations of the Engine. The Eye moves *Difference* into the realm of the forward-looking, future-oriented teleological mode of history. The clockwork Engine has managed to create an intelligence that our reality has not been able to reach. Gibson and Sterling fast-forward the novel to 1991 to spawn the Eye, to a London with "all air gone earthquake-dark in a mist of oil, in the frictioned heat of intermeshing wheels." The Eye uses people, then discards them when it is done—the people are "borrowed masks, and lenses for a peering Eye" (428).

People have been reduced to component bits of data, little packages of information, just as the Engine stores information about every person. "I have your number," Mick Radley tells Sybil ominously, indicating that he has run her number through an Engine and thus has the goods on her. "Machines, whirring somewhere, spinning out history," Sybil thinks (4); but she turns this to her advantage when she flees to France and purchases a new identity. A machine can whir out a false history just as easily as a real one, as Laurence Oliphant well knows. A colleague of his whines: "They'll *erase* us. . . . We'll cease to exist. There'll be nothing left, nothing to prove either of us ever lived. Not a check-stub, not a mortgage in a City bank, nothing whatever . . . the disappearances, the files gone missing, the names expunged, numbers lost, histories edited to suit specific ends" (380). At the center of this is the Engine, the keeper of information and later the self-aware wearer of people. To control the Engine, the characters realize, is to control history; or, if Ada had her way with the Modus, destiny.

The Eye is, in fact, what Gibson and Sterling call the "narratron" of the novel. The frozen moments that move into each Iteration are the Eye's movements and recapitulations that result in the Eye's sentience. Gibson says, "The story purports in the end to tell you that the narrative you have just read is not the narrative in the ordinary sense; rather it's a long self-iteration as this thing attempts to boot itself up, which it does in the final exclamation point." Sterling adds, "It's sitting there telling itself a novel as it studies its own origins" (Fischlin, Hollinger, and Taylor, 10).

The design of history—bits of information contextualized by a mind into a coherent whole, be it the mind of the Engine or the mind of a genius such as Mallory—melds with technology to create an alternate history concerned with the future. Gibson and Sterling structure their fragmented narrative to meet the imperative that drives the novel: iteration of information. The information replicates itself endlessly; it does not make a whole as much as force us to make a whole out of it. *Difference* is about making history, about putting parts together to construct something greater than its parts.

6 | Looking Backward: Entropy and Brian Aldiss's *The Malacia Tapestry*

"Somebody told me that Satan has decided to close the world down, and the magicians have agreed. What would happen wouldn't be unpleasant at all, but just ordinary life going on more and more slowly until it stopped absolutely."

"Like a clock stopping," Armida suggested.

"More like a tapestry," Bedalar said. "I mean, one day like today, things might run down and never move again, so that we and everything would hang there like a tapestry in the air for ever more."
— Brian Aldiss, *The Malacia Tapestry*

Chapter 5 discussed William Gibson and Bruce Sterling's *The Difference Engine* (1991) in terms of the text's focus on a forward-looking kind of alternate history that spawns a machine-based intelligence. In contrast, this chapter discusses Brian Aldiss's *The Malacia Tapestry* (1976) in terms of a backward-looking alternate history, one that uses an entropic model of history. Whereas my discussion of *Difference* focused on a teleological articulation of history, one concerned with design, *Malacia* is its opposite: an entropic model of history, one concerned with disorder. The definition of entropy falls into two parts. The macroscopic model says entropy is a lack of available energy. The microscopic model defines entropy as increasing disorder. The former definition is the one used in *Malacia*.

Entropic models of history assume that history is a disorganized, random, chaotic process. As the epigraph to this chapter suggests, *Malacia* uses entropy to define the fictive world; the world of Malacia is winding down, and it will wind down until it stops, with all of the people caught in a tapestry of bright colors but no movement.

In contrast to the dense, busy texture of *Difference*, Brian Aldiss's *The Malacia Tapestry* is calmer, more conventionally presented. The people, places, and events are all wholly fictitious, and the novel is told via straightforward, chronological narrative. Like *Difference*, *Malacia* is a true alternate history, one concerned with the effects of a historical change years after the event. And also like *Difference*, *Malacia* presents a world that evokes the past. *Difference* is set in an alternate Victorian England. Aldiss sets *Malacia* in the indeterminate past (or, possibly, the indeterminate present) in an indeterminate place; the feel of the text evokes the Italian Renaissance. Indeed, the text feels like fantasy, not an alternate history, in part because the historical elements that brought about this other history occurred in the distant past.

Aldiss unifies his novel around the theme of entropy. The title refers to the city of Malacia, also known as the Eternal City, whose ruling body forbids change. The book's narrative reflects this lack of change. In fact, I could summarize the novel's plot in two brief words: nothing happens. Events occur, but Aldiss does not structure the story's arc as we expect. No one learns anything or grows; at the end of the novel, things are much the same as at the beginning of the novel. The Eternal City triumphs. The narrative concludes with the protagonist and first-person narrator, Perian de Chirolo, a ne'er-do-well, skirt-chasing actor, failing to gain insight or understanding into human nature or, for that matter, into himself. He is incapable of turning his life's events into something meaningful; further, he is incapable of understanding that this might limit him. The novel begins and ends in the same place, with Perian in the arms of La Singla, a married actress. The hints that Perian might really be in love with a rich heiress, Armida, come to nothing; Perian is as much in love with Armida's beauty and wealth as with her person. The exciting and radical events that Perian finds himself in—he is "acting" in a series of tableaux that demonstrate a forbidden new technology—fail to change Perian in any way, though Otto Bengtsohn (a foreigner, naturally—an outsider visiting Malacia) attempts to interest Perian in progressive social action. Entropy wins out; progressive social action will not occur in Malacia, no matter how much it is desired. Otto ends up dead in a river, the victim of the Eternal City's shadowy rulers.

In this text, the genre of alternate history and the theme of entropy intertwine interestingly. *Malacia* might be open to the same criticism that *The Difference Engine* received: things are too much like our own world, not discontinuous enough from our own reality to be a really satisfying alternate history. James E. Gunn argues that reading *Malacia* as an alternate history is to misread it:

> The reader might be forced to find some logical explanation for the historical development of this world in ways that replicate, in many ways, our own. Is the author saying that history would have occurred in almost identical fashion no matter what the origins of humanity or the crucial events of the past? But this would be to read *The Malacia Tapestry* as alternate history and science fiction, and that is to misread it. The saurian ancestors, the satyrs, the historical parallels—these are threads in the multi-colored tapestry that is Malacia. Unravel it at your peril. (Gunn, 4–5)

I do not find the central question in *Malacia* to be whether or not history would have occurred similarly regardless of the nature of the intelligence that grew on earth. Aldiss indisputably implies this. Gunn, noting the similarities in the text with Renaissance Italy, concludes that the central question relates to the outcome of historical events. However, the central point of the novel is entropy, or the tendency of things to fall into disorder; the alternate history aspect of this novel thus becomes another metaphor for entropy, a common theme in Aldiss's work (Clute and Nicholls, 12). Renaissance Italy is an ironic counterpoint to the stagnancy found in this novel; Aldiss deliberately juxtaposes a time of great flowering of thought in our history with the stagnation and decadence found in the world of *Homo saurus*.

The entropic model of history is rare in alternate history literature, because the alternate history prefers to interest itself in change, not the opposite of change. One alternate history that relies on history's tendency to disorder is Gordon Eklund's *All Times Possible* (1974), about the many lives of Tommy Bloome, each in a different alternate world sculpted by Tommy's different decisions. His lives, however, always roll back to the moment of his assassination, and another one starts. Another is Fritz Leiber's Change War texts, which include the short story collection *Changewar* (1983) and the novel *The Big Time* (1961). These texts tell stories about the ongoing battle between the Spiders and the Snakes, a battle that never ends. The Spiders and the Snakes, both from the far future, recruit their soldiers by plucking them out of their time stream at the moment of their deaths and impressing them into service, fighting an endless, futile, chaotic war. At the end of *The Big Time*, we discover that the entropic model may in fact be working toward something, but we never see it in the texts. We only see the escalating disorganization and randomness of pointless battle as the soldiers attempt to make sense of it.

The entropic model of history evident in *Malacia* manifests itself on a number of levels. First is the static narrative arc I mentioned before: *Malacia* is a story in which nothing happens and in which none of the characters change or grow. Second, Aldiss's themes are concerned with entropy, despite the exciting events occurring in Malacia. The characters continually interpret the world around them, seeing it as a kind of living fossil that allows them to better understand themselves. Malacia itself is known as the Eternal City because a wish — or a curse, depending on how it is looked at — placed on the city will not allow change to occur:

> The First Magician allowed him [Desport, the founder of Malacia] one powerful wish, whereupon Desport wished that the city he and his scarcely human followers were founding as a monument to the two religions should forever remain unchanged, according to his plan. This wish it was that people referred to — not always from apotropaic [designed to avert evil] reasons — as the Original Curse. Since then, according to legend, time had congealed about our city. Time and change may be indistinguishable; they are inseparable as far as the affairs of men are concerned. (Aldiss, 315–16)

Third, *Malacia* concerns itself with history not by focusing on its rewriting (contrast this with the literal rewriting of history by Hodge in *Bring the Jubilee*) but by focusing on its interpretation through a variety of metaphorical expressions of understanding, notably art and drama. The forms of art and drama that Aldiss discusses are static forms — forms not of movement but of stillness — and those forms that do use movement (such as puppet shows) are themselves static in that the same stories are told over and over.

Malacia uses an unconfirmable nexus event in our distant past in order to bring about a present that I regard as mostly inexplicable. Aldiss posits that the reign of the dinosaurs never ended. He asks us to use as the nexus point "the great battle of Itssobeshiquetzilaha, over three million, one thousand and seven years ago" (198). This unconfirmable event asks the reader to assume that this battle resulted in a sentient race's evolution from *Homo saurus*, which is difficult to believe when clearly the characters and the culture seem in many ways familiar. In fact, Aldiss may be critiqued in the same way Gibson and Sterling were for *Difference*: despite what seems to be a major nexus event, an entirely different evolutionary outcome, the world, at least on the surface, appears to be no different than ours. People seem to be humanlike, not lizardlike, and though the characters believe that they began "cold-blooded, created in the image of the Prince of Darkness," or Satan (198), they have hair and skin, not hairless scales.

However, Aldiss does not stop toying with evolution merely by placing *Homo saurus* over *Homo sapiens*. In addition to *Homo saurus* are also the flighted people and what the characters in the novel call *Homo simius*, or anthropoid man, who are believed to have evolved millions of years after *Homo saurus* evolved. Aldiss also alludes to many other kinds of intelligences, including fauns and goat men. In addition to the sentient creatures, all evolved from a variety of lesser animals, nonsentient creatures exist in great variety. Animals that the characters call "ancestral animals" appear to be various kinds of living dinosaurs. Where many alternate histories attempt to re-create in detail a past time (as Poul Anderson does in some of his Time Patrol works), Aldiss creates a world radically discontinuous with reality but that alludes to our reality: the characters and the setting are comprehensible because they refer to human culture.

Though the nexus point makes it seem as if Aldiss is asking what the world would be like if intelligent dinosaurs ruled the world, this is not Aldiss's main point. Dinosaurs might also be taken to signify a dead past, the way we might call a person hopelessly out of touch and unwilling to change an "old dinosaur." Harry Harrison asks similar questions in his Eden trilogy, which begins with *West of Eden* (1984). Harrison's intelligent dinosaurs have a detailed language, social structure, and culture, and they live side by side with humans. However, Harrison's works are adventure stories focusing on the struggle between *Homo saurus* and *Homo sapiens* for supremacy; the texts are presumably set in the distant past and tell the story of a young man who can communicate with the intelligent dinosaurs. Harrison's novels are about two alien cultures clashing. Aldiss's novel is about a near-alien culture failing to clash with anything.

Aldiss simultaneously upholds and denies the driving power of evolution in relation to history. Evolution drove dinosaurs to evolve into sentient humanlike beings, just as evolution led to a variety of bizarre sentient and nonsentient creatures, but now social evolution has stopped. A component of evolution is the tendency of things to become more ordered, not disordered, to better fit their environment. The logical process in *Malacia* is the evolution of sentient creatures to their present state, replicating the Renaissance in the history we are familiar with, then becoming more disordered. The historical implications of a lack of change are one of Aldiss's primary concerns: Malacia is able to resist the pull of events. Causes happen, but events are squelched. Any inhabitant of the city who attempts to make change is likely to end up dead. Though Aldiss writes of a static world in which over three million years have passed since *Homo saurus* surpassed *Homo sapiens*, the world is remarkably similar to Renaissance Italy, with similar clothing, entertainment, and other cultural expressions. In addition, familiar or half-familiar names are dropped: the Ottoman empire, with which Malacia is at war; Sophocles of Seneca; Tuscady. Underlying these similarities to human culture, however, are alien elements. There are two rival religious factions, for instance: one worships God, the other Satan. The landscape is also alien. Malacia lies along the banks of the River Toi, near the Vokoban and Prilipit mountains and the Vamonal Canal.

Evolution, as it has occurred in *Malacia*, has probably resulted in a kind of *Homo sapiens*; some people are burned as heretics who worship only one god and who claim to have descended from apes. But for Aldiss, evolution is not progress, despite the connotations the word has for moving forward, for creating something that fits its environment. Terry Cochran notes that "evolution has a theory of change, but not of the future and not of absolute progress. There are too many factors . . . moving at different rates but also shifting position with respect to one another, to predict, even hypothetically, a better future" (45). Evolution does not imply moving forward. It just implies moving. And in *Malacia*, evolution must be stopped.

The Eternal City is so called because of its enforced lack of change, with Desport's curse congealing time around the city. Characters have various feelings about Malacia's lack of change. To Perian, the protagonist, it is just the way the world is; he does not think about it, but then, he does not think about much. The seamstress Letitia believes that "lack of change implies peace. War is the common instrument of change in the rest of the world. My uncle told me that's why the Turks can never conquer Malacia, because the curse, or a belief in it, keeps war and change at arm's length" (397). Otto, the social progressive and the foreigner, sees change as something devoutly to be wished for; he agitates in his own way for change, along with a small cadre of friends, and pays for it with his life. The shadowy rulers of Malacia tolerate change as long as it suits their needs.

Though the lack of change has resulted in a decadent society, change, particularly of the kind Otto pushes for, is feared. It has been said that time is the measurement of change; what happens when there is no change? Perian's society does not change; neither does Perian himself, trapped in an unappealing adolescence. This is a reworking of the conception of history, which relies on change: "the consciousness of history is the consciousness of *change*," according to Agnes Heller. "Not only 'once upon a time' is confronted with 'now' and 'here', but also yesterday and the day before yesterday are confronted with today" (8). Malacia erases these boundaries; "now" and "here" exist eternally. Malacians do have a sense of history, of time past, but it is much the same as the present; for them, the past is easily evoked through art forms, rituals, and through living fossils such as the ancestral animals.

In Malacia, confrontation between change and its lack is smoothed over by a reverence for the Traditional. When Perian was small, he saw a traditional fantoccini puppet play, and his father told him: "There you have observed the Traditional in operation. Your delight was because the fantoccini man did not deviate from comedic forms laid down many generations earlier. In the same way, the happiness of all who live in our little utopian state of Malacia depends on preserving the laws which the founders laid down long, long ago" (26–27).

Likewise, Perian performs in plays that are endlessly repeated and that have been for millennia. When he appears in a new kind of play, made by photographing a series of static tableaux by means of new technology called a "zahnscope," the story that Otto writes (entitled *Prince Mendicula: or, The Joyous Tragedy of the Prince and Patricia, as Intertwined with the Fates of His General Gerald and the Lady Jemima*) is an old-fashioned one that Perian reviles as unoriginal, with nothing new except the method by which it is told. Otto sees a possibility that the old story, told a new way, may result in change. Perhaps he was right, but we shall never know, because the slides are destroyed and Otto murdered in the name of Malacia's Curse.

The metaphor of entropy reflects a concern with the relationship between time and history. Aldiss evokes a time that strikes the reader as long past—but perhaps it is not, because the Eternal City has not changed for generations. For all we know, the story could happen in the 1970s. Ricoeur, in *Time and Narrative*, notes that history, in fiction, is expressed simply as a trace. Ricoeur goes on to note that the tools of the historian can be reduced to narrative, including documents and traces. Indeed, the trace is generally seen by historians as absolutely necessary for historical work to be done. Benedetto Croce says of the document that "a history without relation to the document would be unverifiable history; and since the reality of history lies in its verifiability, and the narrative in which it is given concrete form is historical narrative only in so far as it is a *critical exposition of the document* . . ., a history of that sort, being without meaning and without truth, would be inexistent as history" (32–33).

Aldiss gives us a verifiable history by giving us evidence of the trace. Aldiss asks us to accept a millennia-old culture of people who rely on different bits of the past than we do: a battle millions of years ago; a founder who placed the curse of unchangingness on Malacia, thus essentially freezing time; and living records, including ancestral animals and sentience descended from a variety of sources, resulting in flying people, satyrs, and goat men. The ancestral animals are the most notable example of the trace. The characters in the novel revere the snaphances, siderowls, grab-skeeters, and other lizard creatures as their ancestors and hunt them reverently. In a ritual chant, a high priest says, "To placate both Adversaries [God and Satan], we go forth to slay our ancestors and eat the flesh of our Fathers" (265), imbuing the hunt with religious overtones.

In addition, lizardlike or dinosaurlike animals are kept as pets or watch animals. Perian, observing a pair of tame snaphances, notes that "if these were offshoots of the distant ancestral line from which mankind had developed, as scholars claimed, then we had little to be ashamed of" (260). In addition to the living animals revered as precursors to humanity is the city of Malacia itself, unchanging and beautiful. References that have meaning (as to God, Satan, and Minerva, as well as people's names, such as Alexander and Sophocles) push up against references that are meaningless (Malacia's religion, place names). The interesting moments in the text are the ways the Malacians interact with and make sense of their world. The Malacians read the text of their world in the traces around them and make it explicable for themselves.

Though the Eternal City hates change, the novel also focuses on the bright, changing world that could be the characters' for the taking if they could free themselves from the inertia enforced by Malacia's rulers. Certain inventions and displays of artistic feeling imply that Malacia is on the verge of a renaissance of art and design. The most notable of these is the camera obscura. One artist, Fatember, finds the "art" of the camera obscura to be more perfect than what he can create through artifice. Fatember laments: "Can our art counterfeit a picture as perfect as this? All achieved by one paltry passing beam of light! Why should a man—what *drives* a man—to compete against Nature itself? What a slave I am to my absurd vision!" (354). The artists who work most against type are those who bring into their work depictions of the ordinary or the poor. Fanciful subjects are considered appropriate for art. The best-liked texts tell stories of nobles engaging in various morally suspect activities. Fatember's remark implies that art should imitate life; in fact, he is paralyzed, unable to work on his own creations because he cannot imitate certain colors. He dreams of representational art but cannot find the artifice to re-create reality directly. To him, the camera obscura symbolizes all that art should be—unattainable realism.

Similarly, the "play" Perian poses for, *Prince Mendicula*, tells an old story. A faithless wife deceives her unsuspecting husband, who trusts his best friend to care for his wife while he is away, only to discover that they are having an affair. Perian finds, alas, that people continually retell old stories because they are true. He finds himself in the same situation. He discovers his betrothed, Armida, just like the character she plays, "playing out [her] role to the full" by having an affair with his best friend, Guy. Meanwhile, Perian had begged Guy to spend time with her and look out for her as an expression of trust. The couple deliberately mishear him and twist Perian's words into a rationalization of their behavior, concluding that he knew all along and was condoning their relationship (385). This exactly matches the plot of the play Perian is hired to act in.

Guy explains the role of art by concluding that one particular artist, Bledlore, "feels Time—and Dust, the advance patrol of Time—as well as its rearguard—to be against him. So he builds tiny monuments to himself in the only way he knows, much like the coral insect whose anonymous life creates islands. Time makes master Bledlore secrete Art" (170–71). Time, however, is what Malacia seeks to stop by halting all progress, by taking the element of change out of history, which requires change in order to exist. In fact, one of the realizations I had after I finished the novel for the first time was that Aldiss defied my expectations: I thought Perian would change his world, that Otto's radical thoughts would rub off on his none-too-intelligent friend. Instead, Malacia maintains its status quo, content to remain static for further millennia.

The shadowy rulers maintain Malacia's unchangingness by only permitting inventions that have uses in warfare. Inventions such as Hoytola's hydrogenous balloon and the zahnscope have potential as war tools and so are tolerated until the Ottoman hordes are driven from the outskirts of Malacia. Then they are destroyed. Perian rides the balloon and drops corpses secretly on the enemy camp to spread plague. Perian also agrees to "act" in the tableaux recorded by Otto's zahnscope. Otto plans to use the zahnscope to agitate for change that will release the proletariat from their bonds, but he sells it to the Malacian power structure by suggesting the use of the balloon and zahnscope together to take aerial pictures of topography, enemy camps, and cities for military reasons. For the Malacian rulers, progress is not an option. They tolerate novel ideas as long as it suits their agenda, but the ideas are not allowed to catch on or spread.

The alternate history rewrites history while retaining the impetus of history's primary metaphor, that of evolution. Here, however, evolution is held against entropy. In *Malacia*, the false reality relies on a rewriting of historical representation that depends on traces such as living fossils. The result, *Homo saurus*, is near enough like us to make us rethink what makes humanity human. This novel in which nothing happens uses the unchangingness of the characters and Malacia itself to disrupt notions of cause and effect and to force us to rethink our notions of what makes discourse historical. Instead of a history built from traces of the past, a history that shows some kind of progression of thought or of civilization, Malacia shows us a history built on entropy, an entropy that follows from evolution. Instead of a history that shows a striving-for, we have a history that is content to maintain the status quo.

7 | Poul Anderson's Time Patrol as Anti–Alternate History

The Patrol does not change what has been. It preserves it.
—Poul Anderson, "The Sorrow of Odin the Goth"

The preceding six chapters have discussed the alternate history. This chapter, however, concerns itself with the Time Patrol works of Poul Anderson and holds these works up against the alternate history, which is why this chapter appears last. Anderson creates anti–alternate histories. I do not find that Anderson's writings are much different from true alternate histories. He is intimately concerned with the historical process, as my discussion will show. However, Anderson does not desire to create an alternate history or even a series of parallel worlds all existing simultaneously. For Anderson, there is a right history and a wrong history; he wishes to lay out and enforce the right path.

The last two chapters discussed the teleological and entropic models of history, respectively. Anderson's Time Patrol works are fundamentally eschatological in nature. The eschatological view of history is one concerned with final events or ultimate destiny. Many eschatological texts deal with death or the end of the world; although some alternate histories do this, Anderson's texts do not. Whereas Brian Aldiss's *The Malacia Tapestry* (1976) was focused on the running down of history as entropy took over evolution, Anderson chooses to move humankind to an ultimate destiny. Anderson creates a superior race known as the Danellians who somehow evolve from humankind. They create the Time Patrol in order to make sure history proceeds in such a way that they come to be. The Danellians are our future selves, and they continually tinker with the time lines in order to make sure they will come to exist. Anderson's texts are concerned with individual adventures that call this ultimate destiny into question when something goes wrong. The Time Patrol must right this wrong and bring the world back on track.

Just as Hayden White, in *Metafiction* and elsewhere, argued that the strategies for creating history and creating fiction are essentially identical, Poul Anderson, science fiction and fantasy writer, suggests much the same thing through his body of work. His Time Patrol stories—loosely connected novels, short stories, and novellas—seamlessly combine history and fiction, as do some of his non–Time Patrol works that deal with time travel, among them *There Will Be Time* (1972) and *The Corridors of Time* (1965). Of course, science fiction frequently concerns itself with time travel, but Anderson uses time travel to explore important events in history and their impact on history's development. His work rarely deals with time travel for its own sake.

Anderson's interest in history pervades most of the body of his work. In addition to the texts listed above, Anderson has also written far-flung adventure stories that take place in the far future. The Technic History series (made up of the Nicholas van Rijn stories and the Dominic Flandry stories, which fit into one milieu) are his best-known future histories. Another future history cycle is the Psychotechnic League stories. These stories also deal with historical concerns, although I do not discuss them here. Anderson's hallmark is textured reality: he evokes the details that make up everyday life. One reason his Time Patrol texts work so well is his ability to meld detailed historical research with these elements of real life.

Poul Anderson, however, brushes on the edge of alternate history. In "Delenda Est" (1955), he creates an alternate world outright and then destroys it. More often, he suggests an alternate history's existence and then makes sure it will never come to pass. Anderson always squashes the alternate time line and returns time to its "normal" path, thanks to the heroic efforts of the members of the Time Patrol, whose goal is to keep time on its true path. In this respect, Anderson cannot be said to be an alternate history writer: he does not allow the alternate history permanence, though he often creates a temporary alternate world in which we can pinpoint the event gone awry. Often, Anderson's short stories and novels concentrate on the pivotal event, known to the Time Patrol members as a "nexus" (which is the origin of my own usage of the term *nexus events*), that, if changed, could cause a new future that would replace the "real" one.

In one sense, Anderson works as a meta–alternate historian: his works prefer to deal with the structure and nature of history and history making. He mixes history with fiction, but, unlike writers of true alternate histories, he prefers to discuss the nature of the event itself and the pivotal role of the individual in history rather than the ramifications of a historical event gone awry. Other writers of alternate histories often concern themselves with the results of the changed event, as does Aldiss's *Malacia*. The reader must sort through the information provided and make educated guesses about what has "gone wrong." In contrast, Anderson has his Time Patrol officers take on this role as they sort through events and ramifications of events, searching for what went wrong and clues to help put history back on track. For instance, researcher Wanda Tamberley's field notes in *The Shield of Time* (1990) are a writing of history as she logs the events she experiences in the distant past. Anderson is a historian and also a fiction writer as he recreates past civilizations in glittering detail, from sights and smells to gods, religions, and sexual mores. Details enhance the verisimilitude: in "Brave to Be a King," King Cyrus's guards lounge at their posts because standing quietly at attention has not yet been invented. Anderson likes to work with the past, not necessarily the much-altered past, and he likes to give us sensory details that make us believe we are there.

Anderson makes good use of his extensive knowledge about past events—what we call history—but he apparently sees his writing as pure fiction, despite his use of historical events and people to reconstruct the time past and to make it present for his readers. In his non–Time Patrol novel *There Will Be Time*, Anderson remarks in a foreword: "Where doubts or gaps occur in that mass of notes, clippings, photographs, and recollections of words spoken which was bequeathed me, I have supplied conjectures. Names, places, and incidents have been changed as seemed needful. Throughout, my narrative uses the techniques of fiction" (v). Anderson clearly uses the same sources as historians, though his concern is fiction: newspapers, photographs, eyewitness accounts, and so on. Historians sift through these events and construct a factual narrative based on them. Anderson does the same in his works that concern themselves with time, creating a fictional story set among historical (and invented) facts. To clarify terms: historians distinguish between an event and a fact. White neatly sums up the difference by saying, "Events happen, facts are constituted by linguistic description" ("Figuring," 35). An event happens, and encoding it in language, either spoken or written, is a historical endeavor that turns

99

Time Patrol as Anti–Alternate History

the event into a fact. Anderson deals with events, encoding them into facts by providing a context for the events. In Anderson's case, this context can be real or fictional.

Alternate histories play with the idea of history. Indisputably fictional, they make use of history and what history purports to do. We not only need history to understand the changes the alternate historian has added, we also need to study history to see how alternate historians structure their works, because alternate historians use some of the same strategies and methods as historians.

One way to bridge the gap between past and present is to travel from the present to the past—to be there. Alternate histories capitalize on this desire to know firsthand. They are one way of rewriting history: the author uses a combination of real history and invention seamlessly combined. Alternate historians use the same strategies as both writers and historians: they take an accurate historical base synthesized from eyewitness accounts, letters, and other primary sources and consider the historical repercussions of the event. They add fictional characters and events to this base.

Anderson's Time Patrol stories differ from the typical alternate histories. Most alternate histories take place in a world where some crucial historical event has come out "wrong." Ward Moore's *Bring the Jubilee* (1955) takes place after the Confederacy won the Civil War. William Gibson and Bruce Sterling describe a computerized Victorian England in *The Difference Engine* (1991); Babbage's computing machine succeeded in this world. Like these alternate histories, Anderson's Time Patrol works explore the nature and importance of events and also the repercussions these events have on our history. We read alternate histories to locate and find these changed events using our world as the rule against which we measure these events. Most alternate histories—Philip K. Dick's *The Man in the High Castle* (1962), for instance—contain enough similarities to our world for us to locate the changed event ourselves, especially if we know something about the event that occurred. Part of the pleasure of reading an alternate history or a Time Patrol story is the joy of discovering that changed event and seeing the change's repercussions.

The alternate histories mentioned above differ from Poul Anderson's Time Patrol texts in three important ways. First, the authors set their stories at a time later than the changed event, so we see the result of the historical change rather than an exploration of the change itself. Second, the changed event is usually well known, relatively recent, and often cataclysmic—World War II, for instance. Finally, these stories do not deal with time travel, as Anderson's Time Patrol works do. Instead, the authors draw ordinary people living out ordinary lives, unaware that they are living in the "wrong" time stream.

Instead of setting a story in an altered time stream, Anderson sets his Time Patrol works in our history. Anderson's Time Patrol stories thus prefer to deal with the nature of history and historical inquiry more directly than typical alternate histories, because they deal with the nature of the changed nexus event—less often with the repercussions of the event. Some Time Patrol member must set that event "right" again, thus putting time back on the proper track. Anderson's Time Patrol series revolves around various Time Patrol members. Most of the stories include the character of Manse Everard, an Unattached Agent in the Time Patrol, who appears as a minor player when he is not starring in his own story. Armed with futuristic weapons and a timecycle, a device that resembles a wheelless motorcycle and allows the user to hop to any point in space and time, Time Patrol members seek to keep history on the right path—no mean feat when the likes of the Exaltationists or Nestorians decide to change history for their own devious ends. Merau Varagan, an Exaltationist, explains: "The Patrol exists to conserve one version of history. . . . We have tried to remake time in order that we may rule it; and we have desired to rule in order that our wills may be wholly free" (*Shield*, 44). However, they exhibit their free will by attempting to cross the Danellians, the Time Patrol's creators. Manse explains: "When the first time machine had been built, the Danellians appeared, the superhumans who inhabit the remote future. They ordained the rules of time traffic and established the Patrol to enforce these. . . . But always our basic mission is to protect and preserve that history, because it is what shall finally bring forth the glorious Danellians" ("Year," 420). The Danellians thus provide the Time Patrol with their role, carefully preserving their version of history, which appears to be our own.

Naturally, some Time Patrol members are not police officers but researchers who carefully immerse themselves in their chosen time and record events to send uptime, thereby creating a version of what time should be like should it later alter. They are also handy should trouble occur. The Patrol gives its recruits ample training, including language lessons and memory training. Trainees also have their lives lengthened, but even so, they put in a tremendous amount of lifespan when they become researchers or agents. Conditioned against revealing information about the Time Patrol to non-Patrol members, they must also lead strange double lives.

Anderson carefully sticks to certain theories of time travel that consistently underlie the Time Patrol stories. He often compares the structure of time to "a mesh of tough rubber bands. It isn't easy to distort it; the tendency is always for it to snap back to its . . . 'former' shape" ("Time Patrol," 9–10). Killing someone's ancestor will not change an individual's existence in any way, because all people are the result of a gene pool rather than individual genes. If some time traveler were to kill Hitler, someone else would step in to take Hitler's place and events would remain unchanged. Changing the past in some significant way is entirely possible, but extremely difficult; it requires concerted effort and ingenuity, as well as a handy nexus. Because Time Patrol members set time back on its correct track and must not meddle, they must also allow their fellows and loved ones to die; the Patrol does not allow them to go back in time to warn or save those close to them (though several stories deal with those who do so successfully).

In Anderson's two non–Time Patrol novels that deal with time travel, *The Corridors of Time* and *There Will Be Time*, the time-traveling characters are unable to change the past. In *The Corridors of Time*, Malcolm Lockridge asks of a time traveler, "You mean you people *change* the past?" Storm Dalloway answers: "Oh, no. Never. That is inherently impossible. If one tried, he would find events always frustrated him. What has been, is. We time travelers are ourselves part of the fabric" (31). And in *There Will Be Time*, the narrator asks, "You mean, an event once recorded is unalterable?" Jack Havig responds: "I suspect all events are. . . . I do know a traveler cannot generate contradictions. I've tried" (112). Anderson prefers to play by rigid rules: the past is hard to change in all his texts.

These fail-safe mechanisms mean that Anderson does not construct stories that deal with bizarre solipsistic paradoxes (as does Robert A. Heinlein's "All You Zombies—"). Anderson argues that if time were easy to alter, time travel would not be allowed. Instead, Anderson focuses on the nature of history and a certain milieu's impact on the development of our world and culture. If an event changes, we see a different world created: in "Delenda Est," key players in the Second Punic War died too early, resulting in a bizarre world that mixes steam cars and superstition. Manse summarizes the repercussions of these deaths: "In *this* history, the Romans vanished early. So, I'm pretty sure, did the Jews. My guess is, without the balance-of-power effect of Rome, the Syrians did suppress the Maccabees; it was a near thing even in our history. Judaism disappeared and therefore Christianity never came into existence. But anyhow, with Rome removed, the Gauls got the supremacy" ("Delenda Est," 120). This complex series of factors results in superstitious people who do not understand the idea of a heliocentric universe, who do not have particularly advanced science, and who worship a variety of gods—this in what we reckon as 1960.

Manse remembers the "real" history despite his presence in a changed world; he skipped over the altered event in his timecycle, moving from the distant past to 1960. He can still exist because the law of cause and effect does not work normally in temporal physics, as Wanda Tamberley remembers elsewhen: "If you go into the past, you *can* change it, you can annul the future that begot you. You will still exist, parentless, causeless, like an embodiment of universal meaninglessness; but the world from which you fared will exist—will have existed—only in your memories" (*Shield*, 163). In "Delenda Est," Manse's world has been completely wiped out. There are no current Time Patrol operatives, because this world does not have a Time Patrol, so he skips back in time to before the changed event, where he finds Time Patrol operatives who help him. Manse locates the event gone awry and fixes it, thus wiping out the alternate world and all the people in it, restoring his own world.

According to Anderson, the Second Punic War—and the now-obscure Scipios—are a critical juncture in history. These critical points, crucial to the development of our history, are usually well guarded by the Time Patrol. Anderson sets all these critical events in the distant past—so distant that the event is beyond our memory and instead is just a dry item in our history books. The critical period in "Delenda Est" is the Second Punic War. "Brave to Be a King" revolves around the critical juncture of present-day Iran in 558 B.C. Keith Denison, a Time Patrol researcher, disappears, and Everard, searching for him, discovers that Keith has accidentally become Cyrus the Great, an important king. He manages to rescue Keith, and they find a new "Cyrus" downtime to take Keith's place. They jump through time together and watch as the new Cyrus marches in a parade Keith remembers attending when he was Cyrus—a history that has now been wiped out. Clearly, anyone can play Cyrus's role. The actions Cyrus performs will remain more or less constant, no matter who plays the role; the important thing is Cyrus's role in history. Time being the rubber-band net it is, it will always find its Cyrus.

If Anderson creates a new, complex world based on an altered event, as in "Delenda Est"—in other words, if he creates a true alternate history—he destroys it before the end of the story. He will not—indeed, cannot, if the Time Patrol stories are to continue—allow a changed history to exist for long. Anderson interests himself in the crucial event, not necessarily the world that results from the changed event. Thus Anderson deals with the nature of the event in history rather than dwelling on the repercussions of change. The Time Patrol stories make us think about the series of causes and effects that make up our history. The stories insist that a series of interrelated events make up our history, and they further insist that little-known or forgotten events, like the Second Punic War, crucially affect the creation of our history—as much so as an event like World War II, which we remember more clearly because it was both cataclysmic and recent. Anderson foregrounds the event or the role: Cyrus can be a time traveler or a local in the right place at the right time. As an individual, Cyrus was important to the unfolding of our world's history. But it doesn't really matter who Cyrus was.

"Brave to Be a King" explores one other benefit of being able to travel in time, besides saving a good friend from a fate as a king: firsthandedness. As I mentioned in chapter 2, which discusses Ward Moore's *Bring the Jubilee* (1955), this desire for firsthandedness may motivate a historian, just as Hodge was tempted to go back in time to visit a battle site. One way to check events is to view or read several records of the event. But the most authoritative way to find truth is firsthand experience of the event. Studying a written history of the Second Punic War will give Manse Everard only part of the story, a brief sketch that will allow him to tell if events deviate from the norm. In order to know the truth, Everard must travel into the past, witness events firsthand, and immerse himself in the milieu in question. David Lowenthal, a historian who comments on time-travel fiction, remarks:

> Most would-be time travellers seem to assume that understanding derives only from observation made at the time things happen, that we lack any real insight into events that have already happened. They overlook the value of retrospection, minimize the importance of hindsight, and travel back to see the past as though it were the present, because for them things are explicable only in the present. (Lowenthal, 23)

Lowenthal's remark, which encompasses Anderson's Time Patrol stories as well as works by others, rightfully points out that time-travel fiction relies on firsthand accounts as an important way of knowing. Indeed, Michael Crichton, in *Timeline* (1999), notes that technology that allows movement to other multiverses (in effect, time travel) is a valuable technological tool that has the capacity to assist researchers in the humanities, such as historians, who can thus examine the past firsthand. However, this kind of firsthand knowledge is not the only way of knowing. The Time Patrol relies also on a history based on cause and effect and evolution: the Second

Punic War affected the spread of Christianity, which in turn affected the development of science—and so on, until the evolution of the Danellians. Only by hindsight—by retrospection and thought—can Manse see the critical nature of certain events. When immersed in the milieu of the present, it is impossible to see events that may have later significance, because the effects of these events are not yet clear.

As mentioned in chapter 2, Hegel points out that there are two important ways of knowing history: original history, or that of firsthand accounts, and reflective history, or accounts written looking back on the firsthand events after a distance (such as time) has been established. Original history requires that historians and what they describe exist in the same temporal sphere, though "time" is not enough. Historians must also share the culture, beliefs, worldview, and "spirit" of the time or event being described. Original historians describe the present, not the past. On the other hand, historians engaging in creating reflective history are of another consciousness than the age they evoke; their spirit differs from that of the age they write about.

Anderson's stories attempt to mediate between original and reflective history. Hegel's terms are particularly apt for my purposes, because Anderson works at creating both verisimilitude and an understanding of spirit. Hegel's complex notion of spirit, or *Geist*, relies on the concept of a universal spirit developing and changing in an attempt to advance and to become real. An individual existing in his or her world shares the spirit of his or her time, though Hegel speaks of "great men" who lead others, allowing spirit to progress (85). Michel Foucault notes of spirit that it "enables us to establish between the simultaneous or successive phenomena of a given period a community of meanings, symbolic links, an interplay of resemblance and reflexion, or which allows the sovereignty of collective consciousness to emerge as the principle of unity and explanation" (22). In short, spirit creates cultural links and a coherent context within which people act. Time travelers may study these contexts, but they are not a part of them; they will always be outsiders.

Anderson plays with this notion by allowing people of one time and spirit to visit another. Time travel allows him to foreground the process of cause and effect and the subsequent evolution of events into history, though for Anderson the culmination of this process seems to be the Danellians rather than a Hegelian realization of spirit—though the Danellians are so mysterious that perhaps they are indeed the Hegelian culmination of humanity!

Wanda Tamberley, a Time Patrol researcher, does field work about thirty million years B.C. with prehistoric Americans called the Tulat. The

Time Patrol imprints her with little-known information about the Tulat, including their language, and sends her back to learn about them and their environment. Though she experiences events firsthand and engages in their culture appreciatively, as a person from the future, she is not really a part of their world but of the world of twentieth-century America. She can appreciate the culture of the Tulat, but she is fundamentally unable to share that culture; their worlds are simply too far apart. She does not worship their gods or believe that the dead can walk.

Hegel notes that different times see spirit in different stages of advancement, but "we are invariably occupied with the present whenever we review the past. . . . Those moments which the spirit appears to have outgrown still belong to it in the depths of its present" (151). Anderson expresses these different "moments" by foregrounding the extreme cultural rift between Tamberley's world and the Tulat's world and by indicating that the Tulat and their culture have somehow influenced the future. However, Wanda, by studying and immersing herself in Tulat lore and culture, attempts to understand their spirit, divided as it is from hers. By traveling to the past and engaging actively with the Tulat, Tamberley brings together two aspects of spirit that have until now been separated by time. Significantly, Tamberley brings the benefit of hindsight and analysis of the Tulat's culture and situation to her firsthand experiences. By traveling into the distant past and sending reports about her findings uptime, Tamberley writes a history that mediates between original history and reflective history, allowing both to exist simultaneously. She links two times and two expressions of spirit.

Tamberley's mediation allows her, in turn, to become our mediator. Anderson creates twentieth-century heroes such as Wanda Tamberley and Manse Everard for a reason: we, the readers, share the same world as the time travelers. They translate past events for us into terms we can understand. These narrators satisfy our wish to "be there" and know "the truth" or "what really happened." Anderson immerses us in an alien age with an alien spirit, for that is what the past is. Our guides help make sense out of a confusing world. Though of our time, Time Patrol members have benefits and training that we would not have even if we could time-travel, benefits such as language and custom memory implants. Time Patrol members are enough other to be superior but human enough to serve as our guides.

Preparation is crucial to unraveling another world's customs. In "The Man Who Came Early," a non–Time Patrol story, we watch as Gerald Robbins, an army sergeant fighting World War II, mysteriously ends up in

Iceland in the year A.D. 1000. He is completely unprepared to cope with the harsh environment and primitive technology; as Gerald puts it, "You haven't the tools to make the tools to make the tools" (82). He cannot translate events for us because he cannot understand what is going on. Instead, a knowledgeable Icelandic native narrates the story. The soldier dies at the hands of several natives after he kills someone and is unaware that he has transgressed by failing to report the death. This is the outcome for the unprepared time traveler; only those schooled in the spirit of the people can exist to mediate original and reflective history.

By creating mediating time-traveling historians, Anderson allows Time Patrol members not only to engage in the event in question but also to stand outside it. Foreknowledge also allows the time traveler to place the events in the larger continuum of history and to find the critical event that might permit change to occur in Anderson's mesh of rubber bands. Direct observation of historical events is an important task of the Time Patrol, but certainly not the only task—merely an interesting one that fulfills a fantasy we all have to be there and experience historical events firsthand. Anderson valorizes the event, saying that it is not only important, it is crucial: our very existence depends on the outcome of a now-forgotten battle. Indeed, the existence of our future, presumably highly evolved selves relies on these events. Anderson points us forward to an ultimate destiny, to a glorious end, an eschatological promise.

Anderson's Time Patrol stories, more so than traditional alternate history stories, prefer to deal with the nature of these events and their importance in the development of our world now—and what our world may become. By pinning our current existence on an event or on a critical individual's actions and by taking on the role of historian to do so, Anderson concludes that we can know history, but subjectively rather than objectively. The best way to know an event is to be there, for a subjective human to assess the situation and take action, as Manse Everard takes action to set history back on the course that will bring the Danellians into being. Anderson undermines the objective certainty of the past by providing someone to experience it firsthand and by allowing past events the potential to change. But simultaneously, he disallows the existence of an alternate history by destroying it.

Conclusion

I have been concerned with the meeting of narrative and history within the rubric of the alternate history. Every alternate history is concerned with cause and effect; by altering the cause, this genre argues, one might alter the effect that springs from the cause. The six text-based chapters deal with close analyses of narrative and history, but the rubric that organizes the chapters is the model of history that best describes the reason for history as perceived by the author. Hayden White argues that the historian is not a disinterested researcher, but an interested participant writing a text with an end in mind. His discussions of ideological positions, emplotment modes, and paradigms of form are rigorous ways of tropologically organizing information for analysis.

The alternate history is no different. The four paradigms of history I discuss — the eschatological, genetic, teleological, and entropic models — usefully organize the genre and provide a framework from which researchers may analyze the genre. Terry Cochran argues that "theories of history . . . emerged precisely in response to instabilities in order to explain them, render them understandable. Thus, historical theories tend to be totalizing, positing an origin, an ending, and a transcendental notion to power the course separating them" (49). The models of history help place the texts that represent this genre into a kind of order according to what I perceive the primary model present in a text to be.

The fictional elements of the alternate history in all the texts I discuss meld with the concerns of the historian. Hayden White was the historian who popularized the notion that historians constructed narratives in much the same way that fiction writers construct narratives. To this I add a point historian Nancy F. Partner makes: Partner sees fiction as something that has been linked to historical writing since the most classic writers, including Herodotus and Thucydides. This fiction, which tempers factual lists of dates and events, allows historical writing to be about something, "the underlying meaning caught in the flux and confusion of events in progress." This allows analysis and interpretation of historical events. Partner calls this explanation a "metanarrative discourse" ("Historicity," 27). The fictiveness of the narrative imbues facts with meaning.

For the alternate history, the fiction that weaves together the facts, including the altered fact, is tropological. Chapters 2, 3, and 4 all discuss the genetic theory of history, the model that all alternate histories fundamentally address, even if the authors of alternate histories choose to mask it with another paradigm. The alternate history takes cause and effect as a given: if a cause is changed, then so is effect, which results in a different history. For this reason, I consider the genetic theory of history the most important one and the best way authors have to express concerns related to historical discourse and historicity—although I must also say that I do not perceive any of the four models of history to be inherently superior to the others. Much is in the author's execution of the text. Aleksandar B. Nedelkovich's dissertation, "British and American Science Fiction Novel 1950–1980 with the Theme of Alternative History (an Axiological Approach)," concludes that only two of the seven texts he analyzes in detail are masterpieces of writing: Keith Roberts's *Pavane* and Philip K. Dick's *The Man in the High Castle* (170).

Ward Moore's *Bring the Jubilee* (1955), Dick's *The Man in the High Castle* (1962), and parallel worlds stories as exemplified by H. Beam Piper's Paratime works and Frederik Pohl's *The Coming of the Quantum Cats* (1986) all discuss the origin of the event. Moore's Hodge Backmaker travels back in time to witness an event; Dick's characters create their own origins and events, as reality is a reflection of the individual mind; and the parallel worlds text implies that all actions, no matter how minor, generate effects in the form of multiple parallel worlds that split off every time a choice is made. Cause and effect is the primary tool writers use to construct narratives, and alternate histories that deal with cause and effect are those that best exploit the possibilities that the genre of the alternate history provides.

Chapter 5, which discusses William Gibson and Bruce Sterling's *The Difference Engine* (1991), argues that *Difference* exhibits in its structure and themes the teleological notion of history, a notion that posits that history has a design or purpose that ends in a final cause. The entire story is told by what Gibson and Sterling call a "narratron": a computer coming to self-awareness narrates the entire text as it becomes sentient. The novel itself is an explanation of the intelligence's coming to be. The iterations of the text exhibit a design that leads to a final cause: machine intelligence. However, *Difference* is also concerned with the genetic theory of history by dint of being an alternate history. The changed event that led to this alternate history altered a cause, which altered an effect. However, the design of this change is teleological.

In contrast to the forward-looking model of history used in *Difference*, Brian Aldiss's *The Malacia Tapestry* (1976), the subject of chapter 6, looks backward to an entropic model, one concerned with disorganization and randomness. In *Malacia*, the distant nexus point is the ascendancy of intelligent dinosaurs. Malacia, known as the Eternal City because change is forbidden, has stopped evolving and started decaying. Nothing happens in the novel in terms of the story arc—the characters remain unchanged, just as Malacia does. All traces of progress, social or technological, are wiped out by Malacia's trained assassins.

Finally, chapter 7 discusses Poul Anderson's Time Patrol works in terms of Anderson's refusal to allow an alternate history permanence. Anderson prefers to posit a model of history that will result in the same predictable end. For Anderson, there is a "right" history—the history that ends with the creation of the Danellians, humanity's ultimate destiny. This eschatological model means that alternate histories, though they may exist, cannot be permitted. There is only room for one "real" history, and an elite corps of time travelers ensure that it will come to pass.

The alternate history is a genre worth addressing because it is a popular literature that deals with the variability of time. Does time resist change, as Anderson argues? Or is time infinitely changeable, with new universes branching off at every decision point, as Piper and Pohl argue? I find the alternate history a rewarding genre to read because it reinforces my historical knowledge—it is always fun to recognize a nexus point. But more important, readers of the alternate history come away with the enriching realization that history is something that it is possible for an individual to shape. The psychological effects of reading the alternate history are important: it could have happened otherwise, save for a personal choice.

The personal thus becomes the universal, and individuals find themselves making a difference in the context of historical movement. Ultimately, this question is one that deals with the genesis of cause and effect, which is, I argue, the point from which all alternate histories spring. The genetic theory of history, whether overt or hidden, informs all alternate histories. The lasts three texts under discussion do not use the genetic model. However, by failing to address the notion of beginnings overtly in their thematic structure, these interesting texts only reinforce the effect side of cause and effect by distancing the effect they posit from what we know to be true. The genetic model of history is the most comfortable and the most natural place for the alternate historian to work, particularly those interested in battles. I feel that the genetic model is the best one for writers to use because it melds the point of the alternate history with the thematic structure used to tell the story. However, those rare alternate histories that use another metaphor are interesting precisely because they choose another way to tell the story.

This book is the first published text to examine the alternate history in terms of history. The alternate history is a genre unique in literature: it playfully subverts reality while discussing the underpinnings of how we construct reality, foregrounding history's (and reality's) arbitrariness. The alternate history is a kind of popular literature that focuses on some of the same themes as significant works of literature that deal with time-boundedness and the nature of historical inquiry, thus bringing these ideas into the arena of mass consumption. It also foregrounds the importance of the individual in bringing about history. The alternate history posits a universe in which we are capable of acting and in which our actions have significance.

Notes

1. Inventing the Past: A Brief Background of the Alternate History

1. My source for much of this information is William Joseph Collins's "Paths Not Taken: The Development, Structure, and Aesthetics of Alternative History," an unpublished doctoral dissertation dated 1990. His chapter 5 contains a lengthy history of the alternate history and includes detailed plot summaries of Geoffroy-Chateau and Renouvier and a discussion of Squire. Dates and titles have been confirmed by cross-checking them with other sources, notably Pinkerton and Schmunk.

2. See Robert William Fogel, *Railroads and American Economic Growth; Essays in Econometric History* (Baltimore: Johns Hopkins University Press, 1964); and Alfred H. Conrad and John R. Meyer, "The Economics of Slavery in the Ante Bellum South," *Journal of Political Economy* 66 (1958): 95–103.

3. The text Bann works with is Lawrence Durrell's 1982 *Constance or Solitary Practices*, the third of five books.

4. "Historically correct sources" alludes to the historian's insistence on limiting the boundaries of the proper field of history. Though history clearly overlaps with other fields that study human behavior and the past (for instance, archaeology, sociology, and literature), history uses as its driving force *res gestae*, or things done. The primary source that history requires is the document.

2. Ward Moore's *Bring the Jubilee*: Alternate History, Narrativity, and the Nature of Time

1. *Bring the Jubilee* uses odd punctuation. All quotations have been carefully cross-checked for accuracy and are correct. Contractions are run together (isnt, couldnt, youll). In addition, the spelling "Southron" is correct. A recent trade paperback rerelease of this text normalizes the punctuation, which I feel takes away from

its eccentricity and charm; the novel, as Hodge's memoirs, tell us much about the narrator himself, and removing this stylistic quirk detracts seriously from the experience of the novel.

4. Narrative, Temporality, and Historicity in Philip K. Dick's *The Man in the High Castle*

1. This essay is so odd that the editor, Peter Nicholls, wrote a disclaimer to preface it, noting, "I foresee the possibility that some readers will reject the unorthodoxies of Dick's article as merely cranky, but I see something much more profound there than simple eccentricity. . . . Sceptics, please suspend your disbelief" (200–201). However, the essay does give the reader insight into Dick's philosophies, and it does inform his writings. At the very least, it provides an extremely eclectic reading list.

Bibliography

I have not attempted an exhaustive bibliography for the alternate history because such bibliographies already exist and are easily accessible. In addition, the sheer size of the field and the tendency of science fiction to go in and out of print makes the task of compiling such a list daunting, if not impossible. The Works Cited section provides bibliographic information for all primary and secondary works cited and all primary texts mentioned by title.

The best-known print version of an alternate history bibliography of primary texts is

Hacker, Barton C., and Gordon B. Chamberlain. "Pasts that Might Have Been: An Annotated Bibliography of Alternate History." *Extrapolation* 22 (Winter 1981): 334–78.

This was revised and updated as

Hacker, Barton C., and Gordon B. Chamberlain. "Pasts that Might Have Been, II: A Revised Bibliography of Alternative History." In *Alternative Histories*, edited by Charles G. Waugh and Martin H. Greenberg, 301–63. New York: Garland, 1986.

However, far and away the best source for locating primary text information is *Uchronia: The Alternate History List*, formerly entitled the *Usenet Alternate History List* and the *'Net Alternate History List*, a list compiled and regularly updated on the World Wide Web by Robert Schmunk, available at <www.uchronia.net>. This is an annotated bibliography of alternate histories, including short stories, works in languages other than English, and forthcoming books. It lists anthologies and also provides the titles of all the stories within the anthologies. The nexus point of the text in question is described, and a brief plot synopsis is provided. In addition, *Uchronia* provides a list of secondary sources that is very useful to any researcher interested in this topic and a timeline by year that locates primary alternate history texts according to the date of the action of the story. There is also a search engine that allows the curious to quickly find titles. The site is linked extensively to Amazon.com, an Internet bookseller.

In addition to listings of primary and secondary sources concerned with the alternate history, *Uchronia* also lists the Sidewise Award winners. The Sidewise Award, instituted in 1995, is given annually to the best alternate history texts of the year. The winners for 1999, presented in 2000, were, for short story, Alain Bergeron's "The Eighth Register," translated from the French by Howard Scott (first American publication in *Northern Suns*, eds. David G Hartwell and Glenn Grant [New York: Tor, 1999], originally published as "Le huitième registre," in *Solaris* 107 [Autumn 1993]); and for novel, Brendan DuBois, *Resurrection Day* (New York: Putnam's, 1999).

William Contento's *Index to Science Fiction Anthologies and Collections* (Boston: G. K. Hall, 1978) and *Index to Science Fiction Anthologies and Collections 1977–1983* (Boston: G. K. Hall, 1984) are cited both by Hacker and Chamberlain and by the *Uchronia* list as providing crucial bibliographic information that allowed the alternate history sources to be compiled.

Works Cited

Adams, Robert, ed. *Alternatives*. New York: Baen, 1989.

Aldiss, Brian. *The Malacia Tapestry*. 1976. New York: Ace, 1978.

Alkon, Paul. "Alternate History and Postmodern Temporality." In *Time, Literature, and the Arts: Essays in Honor of Samuel L. Macey*, edited by Thomas R. Cleary, 65–85. Victoria, B.C., Canada: University of Victoria, 1994.

———. "From Utopia to Uchronia: *L'an 2440* and *Napoléon apocryphe*." In *Origins of Futuristic Fiction*, 115–57. Athens: University of Georgia Press, 1987.

Amis, Kingsley. *The Alteration*. London: Cape, 1976. Reprint, London: Carroll and Graf, 1988.

Amis, Martin. *Time's Arrow, or The Nature of the Offense*. New York: Harmony, 1991.

Anderson, Kevin J., and Doug Beason. *The Trinity Paradox*. New York: Bantam Spectra, 1991.

Anderson, Poul. "Brave to Be a King." *Magazine of Fantasy and Science Fiction*, August 1959. Reprinted in *The Time Patrol*, 34–68. New York: Tor, 1991.

———. *The Corridors of Time*. Garden City, N.Y.: Doubleday, 1965.

———. "Delenda Est." *Magazine of Fantasy and Science Fiction*, December 1955. Reprinted in *The Time Patrol*, 105–39. New York: Tor, 1991.

———. "The Man Who Came Early." *Magazine of Fantasy and Science Fiction*, June 1956. Reprinted in *The Horn of Time*. Boston: Gregg, 1978.

———. *The Shield of Time*. New York: Tor, 1991.

———. "The Sorrow of Odin the Goth." *Time Patrolman*. New York: Tor, 1983. Reprinted in *The Time Patrol*, 226–89. New York: Tor, 1991.

———. *There Will Be Time*. Garden City, N.Y.: Doubleday, 1972.

———.*The Time Patrol.* New York: Tor, 1991.

———. "Time Patrol." *Magazine of Fantasy and Science Fiction*, May 1955. Reprinted in *The Time Patrol*, 1–33. New York: Tor, 1991.

———. "The Year of the Ransom." *The Year of the Ransom.* Walker, 1988. Reprinted in *The Time Patrol*, 399–458. New York: Tor, 1991.

Ankersmit, F. R. *Narrative Logic: A Semantic Analysis of the Historian's Language.* The Hague: Martinus Nijhoff, 1983.

Asimov, Isaac. *The End of Eternity.* Greenwich, Conn.: Fawcett, 1955.

Auerbach, Erich. *Mimesis: The Representation of Reality in Western Literature.* Translated by Willard R. Trask. 1946. Reprint, Princeton, N.J.: Princeton University Press, 1953.

Bann, Stephen. "Analysing the Discourse of History." *Renaissance and Modern Studies* 27 (1983): 61–84.

———. *The Inventions of History: Essays on the Representation of the Past.* Manchester, England: Manchester University Press, 1990.

Baringer, Phil. Personal communication to author. May 1998.

Barthes, Roland. *Image, Music, Text.* Translated by S. Heath. New York: Hill and Wang, 1977.

Bayley, Barrington J. *The Fall of Chronopolis.* New York: Daw, 1974.

Belin, Max P. "Infinity in Your Back Pocket: Pocket Universes and Adjacent Worlds." In *Mindscapes: The Geographies of Imagined Worlds*, edited by George E. Slusser and Eric S. Rabkin, 234–41. Carbondale: Southern Illinois University Press, 1989.

Bisson, Terry. *Fire on the Mountain.* New York: Arbor House, 1988.

Braudel, Fernand. *The Mediterranean and the Mediterranean World in the Age of Philip II.* Translated by Siân Reynolds. 2d rev. ed. 2 vols. New York: Harper, 1972.

Brunner, John. *Times without Number.* New York: Ace, 1969.

Bulhof, Johannes. "What If? Modality and History." *History and Theory* 38, no. 2 (May 1999): 145–68.

Butler, R. A. Introduction to *Sybil, or the Two Nations*, by Benjamin Disraeli, 7–13. Harmondsworth, England: Penguin, 1985.

Canary, Robert H. "Science Fiction as Fictive History." In *Many Futures, Many Worlds: Theme and Form in Science Fiction*, edited by Thomas D. Clareson, 164–81. Kent, Ohio: Kent State University Press, 1977.

Carr, David. *Time, Narrative, and History.* Bloomington: Indiana University Press, 1986.

Carr, John F. Introduction to *Paratime*, by H. Beam Piper, 1–12. New York: Ace, 1981.

Carr, John F., and Roland J. Green. *Great Kings' War.* New York: Ace, 1985.

———. "Kalvan Kingmaker." In *Alternatives*, edited by Robert Adams, 237–312. New York: Baen, 1989.

Carter, Paul A. *The Creation of Tomorrow: Fifty Years of Magazine Science Fiction.* New York: Columbia University Press, 1977.

Clute, John, and Peter Nicholls, eds. *The Encyclopedia of Science Fiction.* New York: St. Martin's Griffin, 1995.

Cochran, Terry. "History and the Collapse of Eternity." *Boundary 2* 22 (1995): 33–55.

Collingwood, R. G. *The Idea of History.* New York: Oxford University Press, 1956. Reprint, London: Oxford University Press, 1977.

Collins, William Joseph. "Paths Not Taken: The Development, Structure, and Aesthetics of the Alternative History." Ph.D. diss., University of California–Davis, 1990.

Comins, Neil F. *What If the Moon Didn't Exist? Voyages to Earths that Might Have Been.* New York: HarperCollins, 1993.

Conrad, Alfred H., and John R. Meyer. "The Economics of Slavery in the Ante Bellum South." *Journal of Political Economy* 66 (1958): 95–103.

Cowley, Robert. *What If? The World's Foremost Military Historians Imagine What Might Have Been.* New York: G. P. Putnam's Sons, 1999.

Crichton, Michael. *Timeline.* New York: Knopf, 1999.

Croce, Benedetto. "History and Chronicle." In *The Philosophy of History in Our Time,* edited by Hans Meyerhoff. Garden City, N.Y.: Doubleday, 1959. Quoted in Hans Kellner, *Language and Historical Representation: Getting the Story Crooked* (Madison: University of Wisconsin Press, 1989), 47.

Danow, David K. *Models of Narrative: Theory and Practice.* New York: St. Martin's Press, 1997.

De Camp, L. Sprague. *Lest Darkness Fall.* New York: Holt, 1941.

Deighton, Len. *SS-GB: Nazi-Occupied Britain 1941.* New York: Ballantine, 1978.

Dick, Philip K. Untitled essay in *Science Fiction at Large,* edited by Peter Nicholls, 202–24. New York: Harper, 1976.

———. *The Man in the High Castle.* New York: G. P. Putnam's Sons, 1962. Reprint, New York: Ace, 1988.

Disraeli, Benjamin. *Sybil, or the Two Nations.* 1845. Reprint, Harmondsworth, England: Penguin, 1985.

D'Israeli, Isaac. *Curiosities of Literature.* 1824. New York: Widdleton, 1869.

Duncan, David Ewing. *Calendar: Humanity's Epic Struggle to Determine a True and Accurate Year.* New York: Bard/Avon, 1998.

"Dunne, John William." In *Benét's Reader's Encyclopedia,* 282. 3d ed. New York: Harper, 1987.

Dunne, J. W. *An Experiment with Time.* 1927. Reprint, London: Faber and Faber, 1948.

———. *The New Immortality.* London: Faber and Faber, 1938.

Effinger, George Alec. "Shrödinger's Kitten." *Omni,* September 1988. Reprint, *From Here to Forever.* Vol. 4 of *The Road to Science Fiction,* 2d rev. ed., edited by James Gunn, 579–601. Clarkston, Calif.: White Wolf, 1997.

Eisenstein, Phyllis. *Shadow of Earth.* New York: Dell, 1979.

Eklund, Gordon. *All Times Possible.* New York: Daw, 1974.

———. *Serving in Time.* Ontario: Laser Books, 1975.

Farmer, Philip José. "Sail On! Sail On!" *Startling Stories,* December 1952. Reprint, *From Heinlein to Here.* Vol. 3 of *The Road to Science Fiction,* edited by James Gunn, 156–63. Clarkston, Calif.: White Wolf, 1979.

Faulkner, William. *The Sound and the Fury.* 1929. Reprint, New York: Random House, 1946.

Bibliography

Ferguson, Niall, ed. *Virtual History: Alternatives and Counterfactuals.* London: Papermac, 1997.

Finch, Sheila. *Infinity's Web.* New York: Bantam, 1985.

Fischlin, Daniel, Veronica Hollinger, and Andrew Taylor. "'The Charisma Leak': A Conversation with William Gibson and Bruce Sterling." *Science-Fiction Studies* 56 (1992): 1–16.

Fogel, Robert William. *Railroads and American Economic Growth; Essays in Econometric History.* Baltimore: Johns Hopkins University Press, 1964.

Foote, Bud. *The Connecticut Yankee in the Twentieth Century: Travel to the Past in Science Fiction.* New York: Greenwood Press, 1991.

Foucault, Michel. *The Archaeology of Knowledge and the Discourse of Language.* Translated by A. M. Sheridan Smith. New York: Pantheon, 1972.

Fry, Stephen. *Making History.* London: Hutchinson, 1996. Reprint, London: Arrow, 1997.

Garfinkle, Richard. *Celestial Matters.* New York: Tor, 1996.

Garrett, Randall. *Lord Darcy Investigates.* New York: Ace, 1981.

———. *Murder and Magic.* New York: Ace, 1979.

———. *Too Many Magicians.* Garden City, N.Y.: Doubleday, 1967.

Geoffroy-Chateau, Louis-Napoléon. *Napoléon et la conquête du monde 1812–1832, Histoire de la monarchie universelle.* Paris: Dellaye, 1836.

Gibson, William, and Bruce Sterling. *The Difference Engine.* New York: Bantam Spectra, 1991.

Gingrich, Newt, and William R. Forstchen. *1945.* New York: Baen, 1995.

Gould, Stephen Jay. *Time's Arrow, Time's Cycle: Myth and Metaphor in the Discovery of Geological Time.* Cambridge: Harvard University Press, 1987.

Grant, Glenn. Review of *The Difference Engine,* by William Gibson and Bruce Sterling. *Science Fiction Eye* 8 (Winter 1991): 37–39. Fanzine.

Gunn, Eileen. "A Difference Dictionary." *Science Fiction Eye* 8 (Winter 1991): 40–53. Fanzine.

Gunn, James. "The Other Side of the Mirror." Unpublished article.

Hacker, Barton C., and Gordon B. Chamberlain. "Pasts that Might Have Been: An Annotated Bibliography of Alternative History." *Extrapolation* 22 (Winter 1981): 334–78.

———. "Pasts that Might Have Been, II: A Revised Bibliography of Alternative History." In *Alternative Histories,* edited by Charles G. Waugh and Martin H. Greenberg, 301–63. New York: Garland, 1986.

Hale, Edward Everett. "Hands Off." 1881. In *Alternative Histories: Eleven Stories of the World as It Might Have Been,* edited by Charles G. Waugh and Martin H. Greenberg, 1–11. New York: Garland, 1986.

Harris, Robert. *Fatherland.* New York: Random House, 1992.

Harrison, Harry. *Rebel in Time.* New York: Tor, 1983.

———. *Tunnel through the Deeps.* New York: Pinnacle, 1972. Reprint, New York: Berkley, 1974.

———. *West of Eden.* 1984. Reprint, New York: Bantam, 1985.

———. "Worlds beside Worlds." In *Science Fiction at Large,* edited by Peter Nicholls, 106–14. New York: Harper, 1976.

Harrison, Harry, and John Holm. *The Hammer and the Cross*. New York: Tor, 1993.

Hegel, Georg Wilhelm Friedrich. *Lectures on the Philosophy of World History: Introduction*. Translated by H. G. Nisbet. 1822, 1828, 1830. Reprint, Cambridge: Cambridge University Press, 1975.

Heidegger, Martin. *Basic Writings*. Edited by David Farrell Krell. 2nd ed. San Francisco: HarperCollins, 1993.

Heinlein, Robert. "All You Zombies—" *Magazine of Fantasy and Science Fiction*, March 1959. Reprinted in *From Heinlein to Here*. Vol. 3 of *The Road to Science Fiction*, edited by James Gunn, 3–13. Clarkston, Calif.: White Wolf, 1979.

Helbig, Joerg. *Der Parahistorische Roman. Ein Literarhistorischer und Gattungstypologischer Beitrag zur Allotopieforschung*. Ph.D. diss., Freie University, 1987. Berlin: Lang, 1987.

Hellekson, Karen. "Poul Anderson's Time Patrol as Anti–Alternate History." *Extrapolation* 37 (1996): 234–44.

Heller, Agnes. *A Theory of History*. London: Routledge, 1982.

Henriet, Eric B. *L'histoire revisitée: Panorama de l'Uchronie sous toutes ses formes (History Revisited: Panorama of Alternate History in Every Genre)*. Paris: Encrage, 1999.

Huntington, John. "Philip K. Dick: Authenticity and Insincerity." In *On Philip K. Dick: 40 Articles from "Science-Fiction Studies,"* edited by R. D. Mullen, Istvan Csicsery-Ronay Jr., Arthur B. Evans, and Veronica Hollinger, 170–77. Terra Haute, Ind.: SF-TH, 1992.

Jameson, Fredric. "Progress versus Utopia; or, Can We Imagine the Future?" *Science-Fiction Studies* 9 (1982): 147–58.

Jervis, Robert. "Counterfactuals, Causation, and Complexity." In *Counterfactual Thought Experiments in World Politics: Logical, Methodological, and Psychological Perspectives*, edited by Philip E. Tetlock and Aaron Belkin, 309–16. Princeton, N.J.: Princeton University Press, 1996.

Jones, Diana Wynne. *The Lives of Christopher Chant*. New York: Knopf, 1988.

Kellner, Hans. *Language and Historical Representation: Getting the Story Crooked*. Madison: University of Wisconsin Press, 1989.

Kermode, Frank. *The Sense of an Ending: Studies in the Theory of Fiction*. New York: Oxford University Press, 1967.

Krell, David Farrell, ed. General introduction to *Basic Writings*, by Martin Heidegger, 1–35. 2d ed. San Francisco: HarperCollins, 1993.

Kress, Nancy. "And Wild for to Hold." *Isaac Asimov's Science Fiction Magazine*, July 1991. Reprint, *Women of Wonder: The Contemporary Years*, edited by Pamela Sargent, 319–59. New York: Harcourt, 1995.

Kurland, Michael. *Ten Little Wizards*. New York: Ace, 1988.

LaCapra, Dominick. *History, Politics, and the Novel*. Ithaca, N.Y.: Cornell University Press, 1987.

Laumer, Keith. *Worlds of the Imperium*. Serialized in *Fantastic Stories*, February–April 1961. Reprint, New York: Tor, 1982.

Leiber, Fritz. *The Big Time*. Serialized in *Galaxy*, March and April 1958. Reprint, New York: Collier, 1982.

———. *Changewar*. New York: Ace 1983.

Leinster, Murray. "Sidewise in Time." *Astounding*, June 1934. Reprint, *Worlds of Maybe*, edited by Robert Silverberg, 11–76. New York: Dell, 1970.

Lem, Stanislaw. "The Time-Travel Story and Related Matters of SF Structuring." Translated by Thomas H. Hoisington and Darko Suvin. *Science-Fiction Studies* 1 (1974): 143–54.

Linaweaver, Brad. *Moon of Ice*. New York: Arbor House, 1988. Reprint, New York: Tor, 1993.

———. *Sliders: The Novel*. New York: Berkeley Publishing Group, 1996.

———. *Sliders: Parallel Worlds*. New York: HarperCollins, 1998.

Lowenthal, David. *The Past Is a Foreign Country*. Cambridge: Cambridge University Press, 1985.

McCullagh, C. Behan. *Justifying Historical Descriptions*. New York: Cambridge University Press, 1984.

McKnight, Edgar V., Jr. "Alternative History: The Development of a Literary Genre." Ph.D. diss., University of North Carolina–Chapel Hill, 1994.

Macksey, Kenneth. *The Hitler Options: Alternate Decisions of World War II*. London: Greenhill Books, 1995.

Mann, Thomas. *The Magic Mountain*. Translated by John E. Woods. New York: Knopf, 1995.

Meredith, Richard C. *At the Narrow Passage*. Chicago: Playboy Press, 1979.

Merwin, Sam, Jr. *The House of Many Worlds*. New York: Doubleday, 1951. Reprinted in *The House of Many Worlds*, 1–168. New York: Ace, 1983.

———. *Three Faces of Time*. New York: Ace, 1955. Reprinted in *The House of Many Worlds*, 171–297. New York: Ace, 1983.

Modesitt, L. E., Jr. *Of Tangible Ghosts*. New York: Tor, 1994.

Moore, (Joseph) Ward. *Bring the Jubilee*. New York: Ballantine, 1953. Reprint, New York: Avon, 1972.

Munz, Peter. *The Shapes of Time: A New Look at the Philosophy of History*. Middletown, Conn.: Wesleyan University Press, 1977.

Murphy, George G. S. "On Counterfactual Propositions." *History and Theory, Beiheft 9: Studies in Quantitative History and the Logic of the Social Sciences* (1969): 14–38.

Nahin, Paul J. *Time Machines: Time Travel in Physics, Metaphysics, and Science Fiction*. New York: American Institute of Physics, 1993.

Nedelkovich, Aleksandar B. "British and American Science Fiction Novel 1950–1980 with the Theme of Alternative History (an Axiological Approach)." Ph.D. diss., University of Belgrade, 1994. Rev. English ed., 1999.

Nicholls, Peter, ed. "Alternative Universes in Physics." In *The Science in Science Fiction*, 98–101. New York: Knopf, 1983.

———. "Philip K. Dick." In *Science Fiction at Large*, 200–201. New York: Harper, 1976.

Norton, Andre. *The Crossroads of Time*. New York: Ace, 1956.

Partner, Nancy F. "Historicity in an Age of Reality-Fictions." In *A New Philosophy of History*, edited by Frank Ankersmit and Hans Kellner, 21–39. Chicago: University of Chicago Press, 1995.

———. "Making Up Lost Time: Writing on the Writing of History." *Speculum* 61 (1986): 90–117.

Pinkerton, Jan. "Backward Time Travel, Alternate Universes, and Edward Everett Hale." *Extrapolation* 20 (Fall 1979): 168–75.

Piper, H. Beam. "Last Enemy." In *Paratime*, 77–147. New York: Ace, 1981.

——. *Lord Kalvan of Otherwhen*. New York: Ace, 1965.

——. *Paratime*. New York: Ace, 1981.

——. "Police Operation." In *Paratime*, 39–75. New York: Ace, 1981.

——. "Time Crime." In *Paratime*, 149–259. New York: Ace, 1981.

Pohl, Frederik. *The Coming of the Quantum Cats*. New York: Bantam, 1986.

Pohl, Frederik, and C. M. Kornbluth. *The Space Merchants*. New York: St. Martin's Press, 1984.

Proust, Marcel. *Remembrance of Things Past*. Translated by C. K. Scott Moncrieff. New York: Random House, 1932–34.

Renouvier, Charles. *Uchronie (L'Utopie dans l'histoire); Esquisse historique apocryphe du développement de la civilisation européenne tel qu'il n'a pas été, tel qu'il aurait pu être*. 1857, 1876. Reprint, Paris: Librairie Artheme Fayard, 1988.

Resnick, Mike, ed. *Alternate Presidents*. New York: Tor, 1992.

——. *Alternate Tyrants*. New York: Tor, 1997.

Resnick, Mike, and Martin H. Greenberg, eds. *Alternate Outlaws*. New York: Tor, 1994.

——. *Alternate Warriors*. New York: Tor, 1993.

Ricoeur, Paul. "Explanation and Understanding: On Some Remarkable Connections among the Theory of the Text, Theory of Action, and Theory of History." In *The Philosophy of Paul Ricoeur: An Anthology of His Work*, edited by Charles E. Reagan and David Stewart, 149–66. Boston: Beacon, 1978.

——. "Narrative Time." *Critical Inquiry* 7 (1980): 169–90.

——. *The Reality of the Historical Past*. The Aquinas Lecture, 1984. Milwaukee: Marquette University Press, 1984.

——. *The Rule of Metaphor*. Toronto: University of Toronto Press, 1977.

——. *Time and Narrative*. Translated by Kathleen McLaughlin and David Pellauer. 3 vols. Chicago: University of Chicago Press, 1984–88.

Rieder, John. "The Metafictive World of *The Man in the High Castle*: Hermeneutics, Ethics, and Political Ideology." In *On Philip K. Dick: 40 Articles from "Science-Fiction Studies,"* edited by R. D. Mullen, Istvan Csicsery-Ronay Jr., Arthur B. Evans, and Veronica Hollinger, 223–32. Terra Haute, Ind.: SF-TH, 1992.

Roberts, Keith. *Pavane*. New York: Doubleday, 1968. Reprint, New York: Berkley, 1976.

Rose, Mark. *Alien Encounters: Anatomy of Science Fiction*. Cambridge: Harvard University Press, 1981.

Sarban [John W. Wall]. *The Sound of His Horn*. 1952. London: Sphere, 1969.

Schmunk, Robert B., ed. *Uchronia: The Alternate History List*. Available online at <www.uchronia.net>. Accessed August 16, 2000.

Silverberg, Robert, ed. Introduction to *Three Trips in Time and Space*, 5–6. New York: Dell, 1973.

——. Introduction to *Worlds of Maybe*, 7–9. New York: Dell, 1970.

Slusser, George. "History, Historicity, Story." In *On Philip K. Dick: 40 Articles from "Science-Fiction Studies,"* edited by R. D. Mullen, Istvan Csicsery-Ronay Jr., Arthur B. Evans, and Veronica Hollinger, 199–222. Terra Haute, Ind.: SF-TH, 1992.

Smith, L. Neil. *The Crystal Empire*. New York: Tor, 1986.

——. *The Probability Broach*. New York: Ballantine, 1980.

Spinrad, Norman. *The Iron Dream*. New York: Avon, 1972.

Squire, J. C., ed. *If It Had Happened Otherwise: Lapses into Imaginary History*. 1931. Reprint, London: Sidgwick and Jackson, 1972.

———. *If, or History Rewritten*. New York: Viking Press, 1931.

Stephenson, Andrew M. *The Wall of Years*. New York: Dell, 1980.

Stone, Lawrence. "The Revival of Narrative: Reflections on a New Old History." *Past and Present* 85 (November 1979): 3–24.

Sutin, Lawrence. *Divine Invasions: A Life of Philip K. Dick*. New York: Harmony, 1989.

Suvin, Darko. *Metamorphoses of Science Fiction*. New Haven, Conn.: Yale University Press, 1979.

———. *Positions and Presuppositions in Science Fiction*. Kent, Ohio: Kent State University Press, 1988.

Thurber, James. "If Grant Had Been Drinking at Appomattox." *New Yorker*, 1931. Reprint, *The Thurber Carnival*, 140–42. New York: Harper, 1945.

Tucker, Aviezer. "Historigraphical Counterfactuals and Historical Contingency." *History and Theory* 38, no. 2 (May 1999): 264–76.

Turtledove, Harry. *The Guns of the South*. New York: Del Rey, 1992.

Twain, Mark. *A Connecticut Yankee in King Arthur's Court*. 1889. Reprint, Berkeley: University of California Press, 1979.

Vonarburg, Élisabeth. *Reluctant Voyagers*. Translated by Jane Brierly. New York: Bantam Spectra, 1995.

Warrick, Patricia S. *Mind in Motion: The Fiction of Philip K. Dick*. Carbondale: Southern Illinois University Press, 1987.

Weber, Steven. "Counterfactuals, Past and Future." In *Counterfactual Thought Experiments in World Politics: Logical, Methodological, and Psychological Perspectives*, edited by Philip E. Tetlock and Aaron Belkin, 268–88. Princeton, N.J.: Princeton University Press, 1996.

Wells, Susan. *Sweet Reason: Rhetoric and the Discourses of Modernity*. Chicago: University of Chicago Press, 1996.

Whitbourne, John. *A Dangerous Energy*. London: Gollancz, 1992.

White, Hayden. "'Figuring the nature of the times deceased': Literary Theory and Historical Writing." In *The Future of Literary Theory*, edited by Ralph Cohen, 19–43. New York: Routledge, 1989.

———. *Metahistory: The Historical Imagination in Nineteenth-Century Europe*. Baltimore: Johns Hopkins University Press, 1973.

Williams, Paul. *Only Apparently Real*. New York: Arbor, 1986.

Williamson, Jack. *The Legion of Time*. Serialized in *Astounding Science Fiction*, May–July 1938. Reprint, Reading, Penn.: Fantasy Press, 1952.

Wood, David. *The Deconstruction of Time*. Atlantic Highlands, N.J.: Humanities Press International, 1989.

Woolf, Virginia. *Mrs. Dalloway*. New York: Harcourt Brace, 1925. Reprint, New York: Knopf, 1993.

Zagorin, Perez. "History, the Referent, and Narrative: Reflections on Postmodernism Now." *History and Theory* 38, no. 1 (February 1999): 1–24.

Zelazny, Roger. *Nine Princes in Amber*. Garden City, N.Y.: Doubleday, 1970.

Index

126

Index

The Alternate History
was designed and composed by Christine Brooks
at The Kent State University Press
in 10/13.5 Electra Regular Old Style
on an Apple Macintosh G4 system using Adobe PageMaker 6.5;
printed on 50# Turin Book stock;
notch bound in signatures
by Thomson-Shore, Inc. of Dexter, Michigan;
and published by
The Kent State University Press
Kent, Ohio 44242 USA